THE SECRET IN SANDCASTLES

a *Poppy Creek* novel

RACHAEL BLOOME

secret
garden
press

Cover design: Ana Grigoriu-Voicu with Books-design

Editing: Beth Attwood

Proofing: Krista Dapkey with KD Proofreading

SERIES READING ORDER

THE CLAUSE IN CHRISTMAS

THE TRUTH IN TIRAMISU

THE SECRET IN SANDCASTLES

THE MEANING IN MISTLETOE

THE FAITH IN FLOWERS

Dad,

For all the imaginative stories you told me as a child and teaching me to be bold and fearless when it comes to my dreams.

LETTER FROM THE AUTHOR

*D*ear Friends,

While I always enjoy visiting Poppy Creek, I had an especially wonderful time writing this novel. Not only do we spend time with Penny and Colt—and go on some incredible adventures together—but we see more of Frank Barrie, too. Between you and me, he's become one of my favorite characters. And he warns against allowing our fears to consume us, even in our later years.

Watching each of my characters confront their fears, I'm reminded of 2 Timothy 1:7:

> "For God has not given us a spirit of fear, but of power and of love and of a sound mind."

In today's tumultuous world, I'm often tempted to lean into my worries instead of trusting my loving God who has already overcome the world.

If you, too, find yourself with this mindset, I encourage you to hold tightly to the truths of 2 Timothy. And I'm always here to

talk and pray for you. You can reach me at hello@
rachaelbloome.com or in my private reader group on Facebook,
Rachael Bloome's Secret Garden Club.

Until next time...

Blessings & Blooms,

CHAPTER 1

*T*he windows rattled as thunder cracked across the indigo sky.

Penny Heart scrunched her eyes shut, her hands clenched around the worn copy of *King Lear*.

Another boom shook the walls of her spacious studio apartment, followed moments later by a bright flicker of light.

Penny focused on her breathing.

In and out.... In and out....

Her fingers trembling, she set the book facedown on the Victorian-era chaise lounge, forcing her eyes open. "Chip? Are you okay?"

The large Russian tortoise lifted its head before returning his attention to the clump of lettuce scattered across the art deco rug.

A faint smile tipped the corner of Penny's mouth. "I know, I know. I'm overreacting. Just a little thunder and lightning. Nothing to worry about, right?"

Chip blinked, then resumed munching, accustomed to their one-sided conversations.

"Okay, you're right. It'll be fine." As soon as the words left her lips, another loud *crack* exploded in the distance. Penny jumped, fear rippling through her lithe frame as violently as the slash of lightning blazing outside the tall, unobstructed windows.

Digging her nails into the teal velvet, she whispered, "This isn't real, this isn't real." Her father had taught her the mantra when she started having nightmares in first grade. Over time, she'd adopted it in all uncomfortable situations. And given her long list of phobias, she recited it often.

As her short, ragged breaths returned to a more normal rhythm, she wobbled to her feet. "I think I'll make a soothing cup of tea."

Chip shot her a look that said, *It's about time.*

After setting a cast-iron kettle on the antique range, Penny surveyed her stash of loose leaf tea arranged in colorful Depression-glass jars, deciding on a relaxing blend of chamomile and lemon balm.

She hated storms, especially in the summer. Although they weren't as frequent, the warm air seemed to make the thunder more intense and menacing.

While the water boiled, Penny fixed her gaze on her happy place—a small framed photograph of two young girls building a sandcastle on a scenic, secluded beach. A solitary home perched on the ridge line overhead, as though looking down on the youngsters protectively.

It had hung in the same spot for as long as she could remember. The soft, slightly faded colors lent a dreamlike quality to the photograph, and Penny often let her mind wander, creating elaborate backstories for the carefree pair. Perhaps it was because they both shared the same auburn hair as herself or because she didn't have any siblings of her own—or any family at all, for that matter—but Penny liked to imagine they were related to her, possibly long-lost sisters or cousins she'd never met.

If she concentrated hard enough, she could feel the gentle sea breeze caress her skin and the soft grains of sand filter through her fingertips. Although she never ventured farther than the neighboring towns surrounding her home in Poppy Creek, Penny longed to visit the ocean—to glimpse the vast expanse of cerulean waters that stretched into the horizon, promising unfathomable adventures. But as each summer passed, she'd tell herself she'd go next year. And then one year became two, until the notion seemed forever out of reach.

Sturdy raindrops pelted the rooftop, waking Penny from her peaceful reverie. She was no longer on the beach with golden rays of sunlight warming the back of her neck. Her gaze adjusted to the soft glow emanating from the Tiffany lamp and high-pressure sodium light bulbs that pampered her jungle of houseplants.

While her eclectic, bohemian decor of vibrant tapestries, curious knickknacks, and array of vintage furniture seemed eccentric to some, to Penny… they exemplified *home*. The home she and her father built before he passed away nine years ago, leaving her the apartment and his quirky antiques shop directly below.

The kettle screeched, and she quickly shut off the burner, removing the boiling water from the heat. With a gentle circular motion, she poured it over the stainless-steel infuser resting on the bottom of her gold-etched teacup. Almost immediately, the aromatic steam calmed her nerves.

Leaning against the yellow-tile countertop, Penny watched the dried leaves transform the clear liquid into a sultry amber color as the rain pummeled the gambrel roof. "Good thing we don't have to go outside," she told Chip, who didn't seem to care one way or the other as he moved on from the butter lettuce to the mustard greens. "A little sympathy would be nice," she added with a shaky laugh.

Her cell phone chirped in agreement, and Penny snatched it off the counter, grateful for a distraction. Noting the sender of the text, her lips instinctively curled into a smile.

Cassie Hayward… or *Davis*, rather, as of a few days ago.

Although Cassie only arrived in Poppy Creek last Christmas, she'd quickly made an impression on the small town, capturing the heart of one man in particular—Penny's dear friend Luke Davis. The two lovebirds married in a beautiful ceremony on Saturday, just in time to beat the summer storm.

Normally, Penny didn't believe in love. Or rather, she didn't believe it was anything more than a fleeting fancy before inevitable heartache left both parties irreparably damaged. But somehow, Luke and Cassie managed to be an exception to the rule. And she prayed it would last.

As Penny read Cassie's text, her pleasant sentiments evaporated along with her smile.

Emergency update on Frank. Meet in the café ASAP.

Penny cast a furtive glance out the French doors, cringing as virulent raindrops battered the potted herb garden lining the balcony.

Even though The Calendar Café was only a short walk down Main Street, her heartbeat stuttered at the idea of leaving the safety of her apartment. Penny's coppery eyes pleaded with Chip as she projected her guilt onto her aloof roommate. "Don't look at me like that. I'm not a coward, I'm *cautious*. The chances of getting struck by lightning are approximately one in one million, two-hundred and twenty-two thousand. Which may not sound like much. Unless you happen to be next in line."

Turning his back on her, Chip crawled toward his large custom-built enclosure tucked into the corner of the room surrounded by lush philodendrons and pink-leaved ficus.

Penny caved under his purported disapproval. "Okay, okay. I'll go."

Once again, her gaze darted toward the torrential downpour as she gnawed on her bottom lip.

In the grand scheme of things, *death by lightning bolt* ranked fairly low on her list of fears, behind finding an ill-tempered scorpion in her shoe and public speaking.

Drawing in a determined breath, she tucked her bare feet into a pair of Chelsea-style rain boots before covering her summery cotton dress with a yellow raincoat.

Time to face the storm.

And find out what happened to Frank Barrie.

⋆

*T*he discordant raindrops hammering the café's expansive front windows matched Colt Davis's restless energy.

Although he hadn't been back in Poppy Creek for long, he already heard the siren call of his next big adventure. And if Cassie hadn't invited him to join the night's meeting, he'd be packing his bags right now, despite the nagging whisper in the back of his mind telling him to stay.

Taking a sip of his chocolate hazelnut latte, he scanned the familiar faces gathered around the table, each waiting to hear the news about Frank Barrie.

"I still can't believe it," Eliza murmured, absentmindedly pushing a gooey clump of strawberry pie around her plate with a fork while her free hand fidgeted with a strand of blond hair.

Colt marveled at how, only a few weeks ago, he'd asked Eliza Carter on a date. Of course, it was doomed before it even began, considering it had merely been a misguided attempt to ignore his interest in someone else. Someone who'd openly disliked him ever since he stole her juice box their first day of kindergarten.

But it turned out Eliza had her own secret crush. And Colt suspected he'd been as much a distraction for her as she'd been for him. Until they both came to their senses.

The truth was, he couldn't be happier for Eliza, who had not only taken over the café with Cassie after his mother, Maggie, retired, but she'd also reunited with Grant Parker, her first love and the father of her seven-year-old son, Ben. Given their history, Colt suspected an engagement in the near future.

Another reason to forget his ill-fated infatuation and hightail it out of town as soon as possible. Apparently, in Poppy Creek, commitment spread like sagebrush pollen. And Colt was allergic to both.

"I wish I could say the same." Cassie's green eyes brimmed with tears as she leaned into Luke for comfort. "But he's been taking heart medication for years. I suppose I always knew there was a risk of..." Her voice broke, and Luke pulled her closer, wrapping both arms around his wife as though creating a shelter with his physical presence.

Colt wasn't surprised by his older brother's protective gesture. Luke had been solid and dependable since they were kids. But he exhibited a gentle tenderness toward Cassie that went beyond his inherent caring nature. Witnessing their heart-felt connection firsthand stirred a gut-level reaction in Colt he couldn't quite place. But he suddenly felt itchy.

"It's crazy when you think about it," Jack interjected in his deep, rumbling timbre.

Colt noticed his friend's plate had practically been licked clean. At six foot four, Jack Gardener didn't have a problem putting away a slice of pie on any occasion, even a somber one. "Last year, no one in town knew anything about Frank Barrie," Jack continued. "Except that he was a cranky old hermit who roasted coffee out of his barn. And threatened to put buckshot in the backside of anyone who trespassed on his property. But now..." The several tear-filled eyes meeting his gaze finished Jack's thought for him.

Although Colt didn't know Frank well, he could see how deeply everyone cared for him, despite his crusty, cantankerous demeanor.

Luke cleared his throat as Cassie and Eliza sniffled in unison.

Disrupting the solemn silence, the front door blew open, letting in a gust of warm, muggy air and pelting raindrops.

Fighting against the wind, Penny managed to thrust the door closed, and turned to face the group, her huge copper eyes wide with fright. "Sorry I'm late. What'd I miss? Is Frank okay?" Her words spilled from her lips as quickly as the water cascaded off her yellow raincoat, and Colt's gaze flew to her bare legs tucked inside red rubber boots.

After lingering a little too long on her toned calves, he gulped past the roughness in his throat. He still couldn't believe how much she'd changed since their schoolyard days. Although still tall at five-ten, her gangliness had been replaced with graceful, dance-like movements, bordering on hypnotic.

Impulsively, he pushed back his chair. "He's home from the hospital today. But Cassie didn't want to give us all the details until you arrived."

As he strode to meet her at the door, she peered up at him in surprise, water droplets clinging to her long, dark lashes. "What are you doing?"

"Taking your coat." He held out his hand, waiting for her to shrug out of it.

"Why?" She eyed him warily, not moving a muscle.

In the past, Colt would have found her mistrust amusing. After all, he'd played his fair share of pranks on her when they were kids, including the regrettable Juicy Fruit incident. But he'd hoped his opinion wasn't the only one that had changed since childhood.

"So I can add it to my collection of women's rain gear," he teased, mitigating the tension between them. "If you're done with your boots, I'll take those too. They'll go nicely next to my shrine of umbrellas."

She peeled off her coat, her forehead scrunched in suspicion. Rather than hand her dripping rain slicker to Colt, she draped it over the back of a nearby chair.

Although she'd rebuffed his attempt at chivalry, he noticed the glimmer of terror in her eyes had faded. And he mentally added *afraid of thunderstorms* to the list of Penny Heart's Curious Traits and Tidbits he'd been compiling over the last several days.

"Sit here, Pen." Eliza patted the empty chair beside her.

Penny readily obliged, seeming eager to put some distance between them.

Yeesh. It wasn't as if he planned to drop a centipede down her dress... *again.*

"Can I get you something?" Cassie asked her. "A latte? A slice of pie?"

"A cup of tea would be lovely." Penny swept a few strands of damp hair behind her ears, shooting a sideways glance at Colt as he took the seat on her other side.

"I wouldn't turn down more pie." Jack unabashedly handed Cassie his plate.

"Big surprise," Luke razzed with a good-natured grin.

"Hey," Jack protested. "Is it my fault Eliza's baking is so addictive? Besides, your piece was twice the size of mine. I think you get special treatment since you're married to one of the owners."

"He might have a point." Cassie tossed a playful smirk over her shoulder as she headed for the kitchen. When she returned, she passed out the refreshments before settling beside Luke, her countenance strained. "First, I want to thank you all for coming tonight. I know it's late, and the weather is atrocious. And Liza, please thank Grant for watching Ben so you could be here."

A soft smile illuminated Eliza's chocolate-brown eyes as she admitted, "They're having a great time. They were making a fort in the living room out of sheets and couch cushions when I left, getting ready to watch my favorite musical, *Singin' in the Rain.* Plus, I whipped up some peanut butter cookies that are safe for dogs, so they can share with Vinny. I think Ben wishes we could have thunderstorms every day now." Her vivacious, lilting laugh lent a modicum of joy to the otherwise downcast ambience. For a moment, it even made the persistent raindrops clobbering the cobblestone sidewalk seem slightly more chipper.

Cassie smiled, but it quickly wilted into a frown as soon as she turned the conversation back to Frank. "Beverly called to tell me Frank's prognosis. It's... not good."

Colt crossed his arms in front of his chest, bracing himself for the bad news.

Even idyllic small towns like Poppy Creek weren't immune to heartache and loss.

A fact he knew far too well.

CHAPTER 2

The heady aroma of bergamot curled from Penny's teacup as she sipped the piping-hot Earl Grey. She barely tasted the pungent citrusy spice as she swallowed, intently focused on Cassie's next words.

Ever since Frank Barrie nearly collapsed on the dance floor at Luke and Cassie's wedding, Penny feared the worst. He'd insisted he felt fine, but his pallid features denoted otherwise.

"Frank had a mini heart attack," Cassie explained tearfully. "And because of preexisting conditions, his doctor is recommending some severe lifestyle adjustments. At least temporarily."

"Like what?" Jack asked, taking an unprecedented break from his pie.

"He has to limit his activity as much as possible. Which means…"

"No coffee roasting," Eliza finished on a horrified gasp.

Penny's gaze darted between the two women who'd built their business around Frank's specialty blends. Not only did half the café run off of Cassie's inventive lattes, but Eliza modeled an entire line of desserts around unique, coffee-infused recipes like her mouthwatering tiramisu cheesecake. Not to mention, thanks to Grant's outstanding web design skills, online orders for The Calendar Café's custom coffee blends were skyrocketing.

"Unfortunately, yes," Cassie admitted. "Or cooking, cleaning, and plenty of other activities we all take for granted. Which makes the fact that Frank lives alone particularly problematic."

"He needs to marry Beverly already," Jack laughed, before twisting his face into a more austere expression. "But seriously, I can take care of the cooking. He can order anything he wants off my menu, and I'll find someone to deliver it."

Penny smiled fondly at her flannel-clad friend. A giant bear of a man, Jack had one of the biggest hearts of anyone she knew. And considering Frank spent nearly every Saturday night enjoying a plate of all-you-can-eat ribs at Jack's diner, she didn't think he would protest the generous offer. Although, Frank's doctor may want him to cut back on his red meat consumption. But she wouldn't bring that up in front of Jack. Or he might have his own coronary.

"That would be wonderful. Thank you." Cassie beamed in his direction. "Beverly has offered to cook for him several nights a week, too. And take care of laundry, basic cleaning, and things like that. However, that presents a problem of its own."

"What's that?" Penny leaned forward, her anxious heart sputtering at the mention of Beverly's troubles.

From the moment she and her father moved to Poppy Creek, Penny viewed Beverly Lawrence as a surrogate mother. Some of her favorite memories were of Story Hour at the library, when Beverly, the head librarian, would read aloud to a gaggle of enraptured children. As she got older, Penny would spend countless afternoons at the historic landmark, curled up on the secluded window seat surrounded by a pile of classics like *Anne of Green Gables* and *Wives and Daughters*. There were several occasions when Beverly would lock up late because Penny had been too engrossed in the well-thumbed pages to notice the time.

"You know how Mayor Burns is on this kick to increase tourism?" Cassie asked.

"Don't remind me," Jack snorted. "The other day, he tried to talk me into hanging curtains at the diner. Curtains! Not to mention repainting my front door and adding some planter boxes out front. 'Cosmetic improvements,' he called it. Oh, and he asked me to change the name, too. Apparently, Jack's Diner isn't catchy enough. Never mind it's straightforward and to the point. Can you believe the nerve of that guy?" Crossing his arms, Jack snarled in outrage.

Cassie offered a sympathetic grimace. "I know. He's a little... over zealous. He's working with the chamber of commerce to update the town's guidebook. Beverly volunteered to write a travel guide specifically for senior citizens. Mayor Burns loved the idea, but insisted she include firsthand experiences and anecdotes. But if she's taking care of Frank, Beverly won't have time. I'd offer to do it for her, except I've already promised to spend extra hours working with Frank on the second edition of *The Mariposa Method*. The publisher expects it by the end of the month."

"I'll do it," Penny blurted before she could stop herself.

"Are you sure?" The creases around Cassie's eyes softened with relief. "That would be a huge help."

Penny nodded, although her stomach twisted in revolt. She didn't know the first thing about researching and writing a tourism article. Let alone what activities would appeal to senior citizens. "No problem," she lied. "I'm happy to do it."

"Thanks, Pen. I'm sure Beverly will gladly give you ideas for the list. And they'll probably be easy things you can knock out in a weekend. Mayor Burns is holding a meeting tomorrow night at six o'clock in the town hall for everyone contributing to the guidebook. Can you make it?"

"Sure. That's right around the time I close up shop, anyway." With unsteady hands, Penny brought the teacup to her lips, taking a much-needed sip. Now lukewarm, it tasted sharp and bitter, doing little to assuage her mounting anxiety.

"Excellent. Let's see... what else?" Cassie scrunched her features as she mentally tallied her talking points. "Oh! That's right!" With an apologetic lilt, she said, "Liza, I'll probably have to rely on you a little more around here while I'm helping Frank. Which I feel terrible about, considering we just had our grand opening and—"

"Don't you dare worry about it," Eliza quickly cut in. "You and Luke are saints, postponing your honeymoon and everything."

"We don't mind." Cassie cast an affectionate glance at her husband of only a few days. "I've always wanted to visit Paris in the fall, anyway."

Luke reached for her hand, giving it a squeeze before Cassie returned her attention to the group. "Luke's offered his wood-working talents to make Frank a sturdy walker. And although Reed is out of town at a gardening convention right now, he's volunteered to handle Frank's landscaping needs as soon as he gets back."

As Penny listened to Cassie tick off the various tasks already taken care of, her heart warmed. This was what she loved most about living in a small town—the way everyone came together, utilizing their unique skills to help someone in need. Reed Hollis ran the local nursery, and although he already spent every day tending two acres of lush flower beds, he didn't hesitate to lend a hand.

And neither did anyone else in the room.

Well... except for *one*.

Penny realized Colt had been uncharacteristically quiet during the entire exchange. Not that she was all that surprised. Colt didn't *do* community. In fact, he prided himself on his nomadic, solitary lifestyle, preferring his ridiculous—and often dangerous—adventures to anything as mundane as helping a friend in need. To be honest, she wasn't sure why he was even here. Last she'd heard, he planned to leave town right after the wedding.

Drumming her fingertips against the tabletop, Cassie cleared her throat. "There's one problem I can't seem to find a solution for..." She hesitated, drawing in a deep breath before exhaling slowly. "The thing is, Frank really shouldn't be alone. I realize Beverly or one of us will be there during the day, but what about at night? What if he falls? Or needs help? There should be someone there at all times."

Cassie seemed to go out of her way to avoid looking directly at Colt. Which struck Penny as odd. It wasn't as if...

Oh, no! No way. Cassie couldn't be considering Colt for the job, could she? That would be certifiably insane. Frank needed someone reliable. Not the guy who'd lost their third-grade mascot, Toadious, the weekend he took the classroom's pet bull-frog home. Or the guy who didn't merely live life *on* the edge, he dangled off of it—regardless of the consequences.

No, Colt—aka pandemonium personified—was the last person who should be taking care of Frank. Or a bullfrog. Or anything living, for that matter. Not even a potted cactus should be left in his care.

Penny racked her brain for an alternative. Could *she* stay with Frank? It would mean relocating Chip for a while, but perhaps....

"I'll stay with him."

A hush fell over the room as all eyes turned to Colt.

"Really?" Cassie asked, her lips twitching as though fighting back a knowing grin.

Colt shrugged. "Sure. I can stay in town a little longer. All my stuff's in storage, anyway."

At this revelation, Luke straightened. "Why's your stuff in storage? Where have you been living?"

"Relax, big brother," Colt drawled, slouching in the chair, both legs stretched beneath the table. "I'd planned on taking a cross-country trip after your wedding, so I didn't renew my lease."

"A cross-country trip on your motorcycle?" Luke's tone dripped with disapproval.

"People do it all the time." Colt raised his chin, either defensive or defiant, Penny couldn't tell.

And while she didn't doubt the truth to his claim, she squirmed at the idea. She wouldn't come within a foot of that death trap, let alone ride it across the country. Another item to add to the list of Colt Davis's Catastrophic Decisions.

"Anyway," Cassie said gently, steering the conversation back on track. "That's a lovely offer, Colt. Thank you. Is tomorrow too soon?"

"Nope. Mom'll be disappointed to lose my charming company, but she'll understand."

"Great!" Cassie beamed. "Then I'll count on you to be there."

Penny nearly chortled at Cassie's remark. Count on Colt? The notion was laughable.

You could only count on Colt Davis for one thing....

Complete and utter chaos.

☆

The next morning Colt woke to the mouthwatering scent of freshly baked cinnamon rolls—an aroma synonymous with his childhood.

His father used to joke that he fell in love with his mother because of her sweet disposition and married her because of her cinnamon rolls.

At the thought of his father, Colt's chest tightened.

Flinging back the covers, he swung his bare feet over the side of the bed, blinking in the bright morning sunlight filtering through the handmade curtains.

When the small upstairs bedroom had belonged to him, the curtains were green fabric dotted with footballs and goal posts. Now they featured black and white stripes and mini Eiffel

Towers. In fact, the entire sewing/craft/guest room boasted an extravagant Parisian theme, from the window coverings to the artwork on the pale-pink walls to the ruffled lace bed skirt.

While it was strange to see how much his childhood bedroom had changed, he appreciated his mother making the space her own. For years after his father passed away, she wouldn't touch a single detail, even leaving his toothbrush in the holder next to hers.

After dressing, Colt padded down the creaking staircase into the kitchen, just in time to catch a big whiff of sugar and spice as Maggie slid the tray of cinnamon rolls from the oven.

"I'll sure miss waking up to this smell in the morning." Colt drew in an exaggerated breath.

Maggie beamed at him. "And I'm going to miss seeing that handsome face."

Colt planted a kiss on her forehead before stealing a toasted pecan from one of the cinnamon rolls, flinching as the steam scorched his fingertip. "Are you sure you don't mind me staying with Frank?"

"Of course not, sweetheart. You're doing a very kind thing, taking care of a man you barely know. I'm proud of you."

Warmth spread over his heart as she removed her oven mitts to lightly pat his cheek.

The moment he'd heard Frank's plight, an image of his father's frail, cancer-riddled body and crumpled features jolted into his mind. And while not entirely rational, he felt compelled to help out in any way he could.

Avoiding the repressed emotions fighting their way to the surface, Colt popped the pecan into his mouth, crunching loudly as he sank onto the wicker chair at the kitchen table. "I like what you did with my bedroom."

"It's nice, isn't it?" Maggie said as she poured them each a cup of coffee.

"Now that you're retired, why don't you go back to Paris?"

Her gaze drifted to the postcard of the Champs-Élysées pinned to the front of the refrigerator—a memento from their honeymoon—surrounded by all the postcards Colt sent from his frequent jaunts around the globe. "It wouldn't be the same without your father."

"What about somewhere else?" Colt took a sip of the strong, heady brew, relishing the chocolaty undertones. "You used to love to travel."

He recalled countless stories about her big European adventure after college, the time she brought back the dreaded cuckoo clock from Germany that drove all the men in the family crazy.

As Maggie scooped a warm cinnamon roll onto one of her favorite Blue Willow collector's plates, she murmured wistfully, "That was a long time ago."

"Do you still have the tickets?"

Her hand froze midair, the plump pastry poised on the end of the wide metal spatula. After a long pause, she slipped it onto the plate. "Yes, I do."

She'd bought open-ended airline tickets when his father went into remission. They had grand plans to travel the world after Luke's graduation from law school. But then the cancer returned, a million times more aggressive than before. His health deteriorated quickly, and they lost him four months later.

Colt forced the painful memories aside with a gulp of coffee, wincing as it burned the back of his throat. "Why don't you use them, Mom? You were always talking about vacationing on a quiet beach with a comfy lounge chair and a stack of books. The Greek Isles are beautiful this time of year. You could take a friend with you."

Maggie set the plates on the table and settled in the chair beside him. "Maybe someday."

Colt bit back a sigh. She'd been saying the same thing for almost a decade. "Want me to take you? I'm a pretty good tour guide."

She smiled softly. "I'm sure you are, sweetheart. And I appreciate the offer. Maybe someday."

There were those words again. *Maybe someday.*

His parents recited the mantra their entire marriage.

And one thing he'd learned from his father's passing was that the only thing worse than living with regrets...

Was dying with them.

CHAPTER 3

*S*avoring the scent of aged leather and ink, Penny unabashedly brought the frayed spine to her nose, inhaling deeply.

Beverly's lips arched in an appreciative smile. "I do the same thing and always get the most humorous stares."

"People don't know what they're missing." After checking in the worn copy of *Great Expectations*, Penny moved on to the next book in the tall stack of returns.

"You don't have to help, you know. As much as I appreciate the company, you've already done me an enormous favor by taking over my article for the guidebook."

"I don't mind. Sorting the return pile always soothes me. Besides, Bree keeps begging me for more hours at the shop so she can bulk up her savings before leaving for college."

Plus, Penny missed spending time at the library with Beverly, soaking up the bewitching energy of a thousand stories yet to be explored.

"And why do you need soothing?" Beverly asked. "Is something troubling you?"

Penny shrugged. "Nothing specific. Just a general malaise."

As she shuffled through the old-fashioned card catalog, Beverly cast a sideways glance in her direction. "It wouldn't have anything to do with a certain handsome young gentleman who's prolonged his stay in town, would it?"

"Who, Colt?" Penny pulled a face. "No. Although, if I *were* to find his presence stressful, it would be perfectly understandable. You remember what a terror he was."

"He was certainly a spirited child," Beverly admitted with a soft chuckle.

"You're being nice. I think corralling all of Bill Tucker's chickens in the high school auditorium right before graduation was a little more than spirited."

At the memory, Beverly burst out laughing. "My heavens! I'd forgotten about that!"

"Well, I haven't," Penny mumbled. One of the hens had laid an egg on her chair. A fact she hadn't noticed until she heard the unpleasant crunch when she sat down.

After wiping a tear of laughter from the corner of her eye with an embroidered handkerchief, Beverly tucked it inside the pocket of her lightweight cardigan before handing Penny the appropriate card. "At least there's never a dull moment when he's around."

"I'd prefer dull over deadly. Remember when he set off fire-crackers in the gazebo? He almost lit the entire town on fire." Tension crept up her shoulders at the memory. Gritting her teeth, she roughly slid the card into the sleeve secured on the inside cover.

"Yes, that was a rather dangerous prank," Beverly conceded. "Although, that was quite a long time ago. People mature with age. I'm sure most of his shenanigans have remained in the past."

"Maybe…." Penny trailed off, still skeptical.

"Why don't you spend some time with him and find out?" Beverly suggested, her tone a smidge higher-pitched than usual, as though she had a hidden agenda.

"Not a chance." Penny slammed the book shut a little harder than necessary. "Spending time with Colt is pretty high on my list of things to avoid." Right before poking a sleeping grizzly bear with a stick.

"If you insist," Beverly said with unveiled disappointment. "I only thought with the shortage of available men in town…"

Penny grimaced. She'd hoped to avoid this topic for another few months, at least. After all, it always went the same way.

"I appreciate your concern. Honestly, I do. But you know I'm not interested in dating anyone. Let alone someone as abysmally wrong for me as Colt Davis. The man is a menace."

Beverly's brow pinched together as she formulated a response. Finally, she laid a hand gently over Penny's. "Sweet girl, I love you as though you were my own daughter. And if I meddle, it's only because I care."

Penny nodded, tears suddenly pricking the backs of her eyes.

"And because I care," —Beverly continued softly—"I don't want to see you miss out on your own happily ever after."

"Most happily ever afters only exist in here." Penny flipped the pages of a well-thumbed romance novel. "They're make-believe."

Beverly's pale-blue eyes filled with sadness. "I wish I could change your mind."

Forcing a more lighthearted tone, Penny said, "I'm rooting for you and Frank. Really, I am. But in my experience, I don't see that many couples make it all the way to *until death do us part*. And I just don't think the heartache is worth it. At least, not for me."

With a resigned sigh, Beverly relented. "You always did have a stubborn head on your shoulders."

Penny flashed a playful grin. "Dad taught me to be a woman who speaks my mind."

"Yes, and I'm very glad he did. I just wish you'd speak what's in your heart, too." Beverly reached out and swept a strand of hair behind Penny's ear, a tender, motherly gesture that nearly moved her to tears again.

While Beverly usually understood her innermost thoughts, they would forever be at odds on this particular topic.

And even more so when it came to Colt.

✲

*A*s Colt turned off the main road onto Frank Barrie's driveway, he eased off the throttle, the engine of his sleek, all-black Triumph Bonneville simmering to a gentle hum. Lifting the visor of his gunmetal racing helmet, he did a double take.

In high school, Old Man Barrie's place was the stuff of legends. The entrance, shielded by thorny blackberry brambles and sycamore trees choked by mistletoe, frightened away prospective intruders. Colt and his friends would dare each other to sneak onto the property, placing bets to see who could get closest to the dilapidated farmhouse without getting caught.

Once, Colt had made it all the way to the run-down barn behind the house, dumbstruck when he caught sight of Frank roasting coffee in a strange metal contraption with smoke billowing out the top. Tall, five-gallon mason jars filled with dark, velvety beans had lined a wooden table like soldiers keeping guard.

When the crotchety miser spotted him, Colt's fear surpassed his desire to impress his peers. Pivoting on the spot, he'd sprinted toward the road as though he were carrying the winning touchdown on homecoming night. Until this day, he'd never even considered returning.

Now, more than a decade later, Frank's property looked unrecognizable. The trees had been eradicated of mistletoe and neatly pruned, while the once wild blackberry brambles were carefully trimmed, ready to be picked at the end of summer.

Skidding to a halt in the driveway, he scattered loose gravel at Luke and Cassie's feet.

His brother arched an eyebrow, and Colt muffled a groan.

It figured Luke would be waiting to make sure he showed up. When would people realize he wasn't a foolish, irresponsible kid anymore?

"Fancy meeting you here," Colt drawled as he peeled off his helmet.

"We thought we'd help you settle in." Cassie greeted him with a warm smile. "Frank isn't exactly the most exuberant welcome committee."

"Why doesn't that surprise me?" Colt said with a wry grin. Unhooking the safety strap, he hoisted his duffel bag off the back of the bike.

"He really is a lot better than he used to be," Cassie assured him. "But..." She toyed with a strand of her long dark hair, a tentative expression stretched across her face. "There's something I should tell you before we go inside."

Uh-oh. Colt didn't like the sound of that. "What's up?"

"Well..." She glanced at Luke before returning her gaze to Colt. "I may have told Frank a tiny fib, so he'd agree to this arrangement. As you might suspect, he's not great at accepting help. Even when he needs it."

"What kind of fib?" Colt shifted the duffel to his other shoulder, wondering what he'd gotten himself into.

"I told him that *you* were the one who needed help," she admitted sheepishly.

Colt blinked in surprise. "Me?"

Cassie nodded, biting her bottom lip.

"What kind of help?" he asked tentatively.

"Well..." Once again, her gaze darted to Luke, and Colt wondered just how big of a role his brother played in all of this. "I told Frank that you're... a little aimless. And he'd be doing us a huge favor if he took you in and taught you a trade."

"A trade?" Colt repeated, reality sinking in. "I suppose you mean like coffee roasting?"

"Yes," Cassie confessed with an apologetic grimace. "I'm sorry. It seemed like a good idea at the time. But if you'd rather I tell him—"

"It's fine." Colt waved away her concern. "If that's what it takes for him to agree to this whole thing, I'm cool with it."

"Thank you, thank you! You have no idea how much this means to us." Her voice thick with emotion, Cassie threw her arms around Colt's neck, hugging him tightly.

"No problem," he mumbled, awkwardly patting her back.

While he didn't relish the idea of roasting coffee, it was good for Frank to have a purpose—something to focus on besides his ailing health.

Besides, in a way, Frank *was* doing him a favor by giving him a reason to stick around. While he'd never admit it—even to himself—Colt wasn't ready to leave town quite yet.

Something about being a part of a community again compelled him to stay. Even though he knew it couldn't last.

Not if he wanted to fulfill his father's dying wish.

CHAPTER 4

*F*rank's glower pinned Colt to the scuffed pine floorboards. He might be confined to a comfortable recliner, but he hadn't lost the fight in his intense steel-gray eyes.

"So, you're the rabble-rouser?" Frank's thick, peppery eyebrows lowered even further.

Colt stiffened. Rabble-rouser seemed like a far cry from aimless. What exactly had Cassie told him?

"Colt Davis, sir. It's nice to officially meet you." Colt extended his hand, but as Frank's menacing eyes narrowed into slits, he immediately retracted it, clearing his throat more loudly than he intended.

"I know who you are," Frank growled. "You're the nuisance who used to trespass on my land."

Colt's gaze darted to Luke and Cassie for backup. The ole curmudgeon had a pretty sharp memory for a man his age. And a sharp tongue, too.

"Why don't I put on a pot of decaf?" Cassie cut in quickly, a tad more chipper than the situation warranted.

"Decaf is the devil's brew," Frank grumbled.

"Doctor's orders," Cassie quipped. "But if you promise to be civil, I'll make half-caff."

Frank mumbled again, but Cassie must have interpreted the unintelligible sound as compliance because she spun on her heel, a satisfied smile illuminating her features.

"I'll help." Luke shot an encouraging glance at Colt before disappearing down the hallway after his wife.

Left alone with Frank, Colt's pulse spiked. He felt like a quarterback clutching the ball, deserted by his offensive linemen. His fight-or-flight instincts were finely honed to flight, but in this case, he stood his ground.

Frank lifted the hulking tome of *War and Peace* draped over the arm of the recliner and focused his attention on the yellowed pages. Without glancing up, he gestured toward the worn leather sofa. "Have a seat. Unless you're fond of that particular spot on the floor."

Unsettled by Frank's unexpected attempt at humor, Colt hesitated a moment before sinking into the plump cushions. Running a hand over the soft, supple upholstery—presumably broken in by age and frequent use—he surveyed his surroundings.

The classic bones of the farmhouse had to be over a hundred years old, and the sturdy structure had maintained its rustic charm. Thick, heavy drapes were drawn back, casting late afternoon sunlight across the dark, masculine furnishings. The only items not congruent with Frank's gruff exterior were the gobs of floral arrangements sprouting from every nook and cranny.

"Nice flowers." Colt nodded toward a bouquet of white roses and golden-hued gardenias with a notecard peeking from the fragrant foliage imparting well wishes for a speedy recovery.

"It looks like a funeral parlor in here," Frank grunted, wrinkling his nose in disapproval. "I'm dying, not dead."

"You're not dying, either," Colt corrected emphatically.

Cassie had assured everyone at last night's meeting that although Frank's condition needed careful monitoring over the next several weeks, his doctor expected a full recovery if the unruly patient could give his body enough time to heal.

Frank opened his mouth—probably to argue—but snapped it shut when Cassie swept into the room carrying a wooden tray topped with stoneware mugs, a mismatched creamer and sugar bowl, and a French press containing piping-hot coffee. Luke followed with a heaping plate of raspberry mocha scones Colt recognized as one of Eliza's many specialties at The Calendar Café.

"Glad to see you two getting along." Cassie flashed an overly optimistic smile as she slid the tray onto the coffee table. After she handed Frank a wide-brimmed mug, she settled on the far end of the couch, nestling against Luke as he hooked one arm around her shoulders.

"So, how are you?" Luke asked Frank, attempting to fill the conspicuous silence.

"Peachy." Frank took his first sip, the lines etched into his forehead detailing exactly what he thought of the doctor's recommendation to drink decaf.

"Can we get you something from Jack's for dinner tonight?" Cassie asked.

"I usually get the all-you-can-eat ribs. But since my house arrest prohibits me from going back for seconds..." Frank trailed off as a murky shadow clouded his countenance.

Colt shifted his weight, a knot of sympathy twisting in his gut. As someone who never stayed in one country for very long, let alone trapped in the same house, he bristled on Frank's behalf.

"I guess the tri-tip special would be fine," Frank said after a pause.

"How about something a little more heart-healthy?" Cassie pressed gently. "Like the barbecue chicken?"

Frank scowled.

"I can cook something," Colt offered impulsively.

"You can?" Cassie tilted her head, studying him with newfound curiosity.

"Sure. I went to culinary school."

"Only for two semesters," Luke added.

"Have *you* ever poached an egg?" Colt countered in mock offense.

"You have a point," his brother chuckled.

"I never cared for poached eggs. All that orange goo oozing everywhere." Frank shuddered.

Colt grinned, undeterred. "I can make whatever you want."

The old man eyed him over the rim of his mug. "How about shish kebab? Authentic, like my Armenian mother used to make."

"Frank, I didn't know you were Armenian," Luke said with interest.

"On my mother's side. My father was more of a Heinz 57."

"What does that mean?" Cassie asked.

"A little bit of everything," Colt told her, his lips quirked. Turning to Frank, he added, "Consider it done." While he'd only completed two semesters, he'd continued learning on his own, favoring French and Middle Eastern cuisine. If Frank wanted authentic Armenian shish kebab, that's exactly what he'd get.

But for all Colt's confidence, Frank didn't look convinced. Although, he *did* look resigned. And Colt wasn't sure which emotion he found the most troubling.

"Great. This is going to work out perfectly." Cassie smiled as she nuzzled closer to Luke.

"But I can't make it tonight," Colt said quickly.

"I knew it," Frank muttered. "You don't know how."

"Oh, I know how." Colt took a slow, languorous sip before lowering the mug, resting it on his knee. "But traditional shish kebab takes two or three days to marinate. It'll be ready by the weekend."

A brief flicker of surprise flashed across Frank's weathered features. But only for a moment. Leveling his gaze on Colt, he added, "Don't forget the pilaf."

"I wouldn't dream of it." Leaning forward, Colt set his mug on the coffee table and reached for the French press. Slow and steady, he poured himself another serving, steam wafting from the spout.

Frank Barrie may not want his help right now, but sooner or later, Colt would crack through his crusty shell and show him it wasn't too late to live his life to the fullest.

The way his father would have...

If he'd had time.

⭐

*P*enny's stomach fluttered as she stepped into the expansive one-room town hall. Since it doubled as an art and dance studio by day and rehearsal space for the local theater group by night, the decor was eclectic to say the least. Amateurish landscape paintings bedecked the pine slat walls beside posters announcing One Night Only, Shakespeare in the Park.

Her gaze traveled past a rolling rack of Renaissance-era costumes to a long folding table teeming with tantalizing desserts.

The flutter in her stomach transformed into a low, rumbling growl. And the plump, oversize brownies seemed to be calling her name.

"Be careful with those. They're not what you think."

The rich, toe-curling timbre sent goose bumps skittering across her arms. Penny hated how the all-too-familiar voice made her knees quake. She blamed the phenomena on faulty biology.

Squaring her shoulders, she whirled around to face the annoyingly affable grin of Colt Davis, which was only made more vexing by the dimple in his left cheek. It simply wasn't fair that such appealing features belonged to such a disagreeable man-child. "What are *you* doing here?"

Ignoring her question, Colt filled his plate with every dessert *except* the brownies. "They look like regular brownies, but don't be fooled. They've got some kick. Cayenne pepper would be my guess." He pulled a face.

"You don't like spicy food?" she asked, making a point to grab one of the offending treats.

"More like spicy food doesn't like me."

"Hmm... I can't imagine why," she smirked.

Chuckling, Colt stuffed a powdered doughnut hole in his mouth and slowly licked his fingers.

Something about the gesture grated on her nerves. Folding her arms in front of her chest, Penny persisted. "So, what *are* you doing here? Aren't you supposed to be with Frank?"

"Beverly came over to cook him dinner and watch *Wheel of Fortune*, so I thought I'd give them some privacy. Plus, Mayor Burns left a strangely urgent voice mail insisting I show up tonight."

Penny frowned. Why would the mayor want Colt to attend the meeting? With all the times he'd had to clean up after Colt's antics, she was surprised he hadn't declared the day Colt left for college a town holiday.

Before she could press further, Mayor Burns whacked his gavel against the podium. Penny jumped in surprise, and to her annoyance, Colt laughed.

Jutting her chin in the air, she spun on her heel, making her way to the back row of folding chairs. Determined not to let him get under her skin, she stared straight ahead as he chose the chair next to her.

Through most of the mayor's long-winded speech, Penny shifted in her seat, scooting farther away from Colt's encroaching thigh. Was it absolutely necessary for him to sit so close?

Distracted by his obnoxiously loud chewing, she struggled to concentrate on all the talking points, eager not to miss the mysterious reason for Colt's presence. Maybe the mayor was playing a prank, knowing how much Colt loathed meetings of any kind, but especially ones this drawn out and boring. She almost snickered at the thought.

"Hmm... Let's see..." Burns glanced at his notes, his jet-black, overly gelled hair not moving a millimeter as he inclined his head. "Next we have Beverly's article on the top activities in Poppy Creek for senior citizens." Strumming his well-manicured fingernails against the wooden podium, he searched the dozen or so faces staring back at him. "Is Penny Heart here?"

"I'm here." Penny raised her hand in the back row, suddenly self-conscious as everyone turned to stare.

"Wonderful." Burns flashed his unnaturally white teeth. "I've been informed you're taking over for Beverly, which is excellent, since I've decided to go in a different direction."

"A different direction?" Penny repeated, her fists curling around the soft cotton folds of her vintage, pink-gingham sundress.

"I liked Beverly's proposal, but I'd rather appeal to a more exciting crowd. Younger blood, if you will. The new title for your article is 'Poppy Creek's Top 5 Thrilling Summer Adventures.' While I'd like the activities to be summery—think outdoorsy— they can be available year-round or a special one-day event. But the one criterion that's nonnegotiable is each activity must be exciting! Something to give tourists a real thrill. Great idea, right?" With his smug smile on full display, he looked rather pleased with himself as he waited for her response.

But Penny had lost the ability to speak. Suddenly, all the air evaporated from her lungs. And the temperature in the room escalated by a few hundred degrees.

He must have noticed her flushed features because he asked, "That's not a problem, is it?"

"N-no, no problem," she stammered, her head swimming.

"Good. Because I want this article to take up a significant portion of the guidebook. Which is also why I've arranged for you to have some help."

The room started to spin in slow motion as Burns shifted his gaze to the chair beside her.

No... this can't be happening.... Penny sucked in a horrified breath.

"Me?" Colt balked, sounding equally astonished.

"You're the resident adventure expert," Burns told him with a devilish grin, as though he enjoyed watching Colt squirm. "There isn't a single hair-raising activity within a hundred miles you haven't tackled with zeal."

"Yeah, but—"

"So, what better person for the job? Penny, of course, will write the article. And it'll be nice to have an outsider's perspective. But you'll supply the knowledge and credibility the article needs. Any objections?"

Before either of them had a chance to respond, Burns slammed his gavel. "Perfect. Moving on to the next order of business...."

But Penny could no longer hear him as wailing alarms resounded inside her head. How had so many things gone so spectacularly wrong in a matter of minutes?

Thrilling, *adventure,* and *Colt* were three words she never wanted strung together in the same sentence.

At least, not where *she* was concerned.

How on earth could she get out of this?

CHAPTER 5

*B*y the time Penny had extricated herself from the meeting and made it back to her apartment, she was close to hyperventilating. Each breath came in short, rapid bursts and left her more winded than before.

It had to be a bad dream and she'd wake up any second.

Flicking on the faucet to fill the teakettle, she cupped a handful of water from the spout, lapping the cool, crisp liquid from her palm. As it soothed the back of her throat, tension slowly melted from her shoulders.

As a child, Penny often refused to drink enough water, preferring apple juice or chocolate milk. So her father hatched a plan, claiming her least favorite beverage contained magical molecules that gave little girls extra strength and smarts. Since she wanted to explore the world one day, like the children in *Swiss Family Robinson* and *Treasure Island*, Penny guzzled up the white lie *and* her weight in water.

Although a small smile curled the edges of her lips at the memory, her chest ached. She missed her father every day, but especially when she needed his calming words of wisdom.

While most people in town viewed Timothy Heart as a timid,

reclusive man, Penny knew the truth. Her father had more adventures in his lifetime than the average person could even fathom—they simply took place in his imagination. He could turn the tiniest, most unremarkable object, like an insignificant, rusty thimble, into an epic tale about a Spanish princess captured by pirates who earned her freedom stitching a battered sail, thus saving the entire crew from a deadly storm on the high seas.

Tears pricking her eyes, Penny glanced toward the far end of the room. A hidden door painted the same antique white as the neighboring walls—including the doorknob—beckoned her.

Switching off the stove's burner, she abandoned her teakettle to cross the creaking elm-wood floorboards. The camouflaged handle groaned, protesting the firm flick of her wrist.

Like the front door, this frame had also become warped with age, and Penny leaned against it with her shoulder, giving it a forceful nudge. As it jerked open, light from the main living area flooded the modest bedroom, which had been added onto the apartment when Penny turned thirteen. Before then, they'd shared the expansive studio, partitioning off large sections with colorful drapes and tapestries. On any given day, they would pretend to be Arabian royalty or explorers on safari. Penny loved their cozy, whimsical home. And even though many people in town encouraged Timothy to buy a "real" house, he'd refused, opting to build the addition instead, turning it into his bedroom that doubled as an office.

Penny's gaze traveled the built-in floor-to-ceiling mahogany bookcases overflowing with dusty, well-worn classics like *The Count of Monte Cristo* and *The Call of the Wild*. As her vision blurred with unshed tears, she glossed over the iron-frame twin bed and Hogarth chair and landed on the mid-nineteenth-century campaign desk.

Growing up, she'd been fascinated with the exquisite piece of history. Due in part to the fantastical story her dad concocted about an army general in love with the daughter of his rival.

But mostly because of the secret compartment.

Scooting it away from the wall, she ran a hand along the back upper edge. Her breath hitched when her fingertips brushed across a familiar engraving. With one quick tap, a hidden drawer popped open at the front of the desk revealing an ordinary white envelope.

A sob caught in her throat as she read the simple inscription scrawled in her father's sloping script.

Sweet P.

The *P* stood for Penny, and he'd called her by the endearment ever since she could remember. Oh, how she longed to hear him say it just one more time. And wrap herself in the comfort and contentment of being unconditionally loved and cherished.

That's why she still hadn't opened the letter—the one she'd found hidden in the desk the day after he died.

Once she broke the seal, she'd lose her last remaining connection to her father. Right now, everything else belonged in the past, merely a memory. But the letter? It could live in the future. As long as she held on to it, not knowing what words it contained, her dad still had something to tell her, perhaps a piece of wisdom to impart.

Whenever she missed him so much she could barely breathe, she'd pull out the envelope. Simply holding it in her hands drew him closer. She could hear his voice, rich and gravelly like a scratched vinyl spinning round and round on their old gramophone as he regaled her with one of his imaginative fairy tales. And if she closed her eyes tightly enough, she could inhale his scent—vintage wool, aged leather, and sandalwood.

Deep down, she knew she'd have to read it someday. But until that day came, she'd relish the connection, no matter how fleeting.

In her lowest moments, it always lifted her spirits.

And tonight, she didn't think she could sink any lower.

*S*ome things never changed.

All throughout high school, Mayor Burns made it his personal mission to break Colt's spirits, claiming he had a zero-tolerance policy for negligent behavior like reckless pranks. Or *buffoonery*, as Burns so eloquently described it.

Of course, the mayor's narrow-mindedness regarding fun and games only encouraged Colt to get more creative. Which usually played out in the same way—a cat-and-mouse game of elaborate hijinks and uninspired punishments. Like the time Burns ordered him to pick up trash for an entire summer after a confetti-cannon stunt gone wrong.

But he'd never been able to tie Colt to the Great Chicken Incident the day of graduation. Was it possible he'd waited all this time for payback?

Colt shook his head in disbelief. *Nah... that'd be crazy.* But still, Burns's latest move had gone too far. And as an adult... *this* time, he could refuse to play along.

Although, spending time with a woman as beautiful as Penny Heart wasn't exactly torture. And the assignment *was* right up his alley. A few weeks filled with adrenaline-inducing adventures paid for by the chamber of commerce? Maybe he was looking at this all wrong.

Maybe ole Burnsy had actually done him a favor.

Seeing the situation in a new light, Colt's weighted footsteps lifted as he made his way to Jack's Diner for one of his friend's famous sarsaparilla floats.

He cracked a smile as he took in the bare-bones exterior, recalling Jack's complaint regarding Mayor Burn's suggested "improvements." The place was far from being an eyesore, with lush English ivy ambling up the ruddy brick walls, but Burns might have a point. Especially when it came to the name. While it may have started out as a diner, over the years, Jack had added a spacious back patio with ample event seating, a large smoker, and two barbecue pits. And his menu had grown. Sure, his humble, down-home friend may not want to admit it, but he'd built himself an incredibly successful restaurant.

A cowbell jangled overhead as Colt pushed through the front door, instantly bombarded by the sweet-and-spicy scent of Jack's signature barbecue sauce.

Jack glanced up from the bar where he carefully dried large soda fountain glasses, sliding them on the shelf behind him.

"Might as well keep one of those out for me," Colt told him with a grin, hopping onto the cracked leather barstool. "Gimme the usual."

Never in one place long enough to have a "usual" anything, Colt liked the way it rolled off the tongue.

"Coming right up." Behind the bar, Jack scooped three enormous mounds of his in-house bourbon vanilla ice cream into the tall glass before popping the top off an ice-cold sarsaparilla. "Are you here to pick up dinner for your new roomie?"

"Har-har," Colt muttered as Jack poured the soda over the ice cream. Delicious fizz bubbled to the surface. It tasted a million times better than a regular root beer float, and Colt had missed the nostalgic indulgence. The faint licorice flavor reminded him of home. "He's having dinner with Beverly. So, I'm on my own tonight."

Shaking his head, Jack stuck a long soda spoon and an oversize straw into the glass before sliding the float across the counter toward Colt. "Who would've thought crotchety ole Frank Barrie would land himself a good woman before either of us?" Chuckling, he added, "Well, before *me*, anyway. We both know you're a die-hard bachelor."

"Proudly." Colt raised his float in a salute. "So, are you going to take my dinner order sometime today? Or do I have to climb back there and make it myself?"

"As if I'd let you set one foot in my kitchen! You'd probably do something ridiculous like julienne a carrot. We *chop* things around here. Or if we're feeling really fancy, we might dice."

"In that case, I'll take one of your pulled pork sandwiches, fries, and an extra-large serving of your barbecue sauce."

Pushing through the swinging door that led to the kitchen, Jack yelled, "Johnson, give me a Big Bad Wolf, a haystack, and a bucket of the mother lode."

Listening in bemusement, Colt slurped his float until Jack returned. "Was that even English?"

"Diner lingo. It helps us keep track of the orders."

"By the time you memorize all that gibberish, couldn't you just memorize the *actual* menu?"

"I wouldn't expect such a refined culinary student to understand," Jack goaded, plucking the dish towel from the counter to resume drying.

"Nor would I want to," Colt countered with a laugh, scooping a spoonful of thick, frothy ice cream.

For the next few minutes, he enjoyed his float in silence, serenaded by the sounds of chatter supplied by the surplus of patrons, numerous clinking glasses, and the subdued country music funneled through speakers mounted in the wood plank ceiling. It figured Jack would decorate the place exactly like his own home—rustic charm without all the charm. The only elements not made of reclaimed wood, metal, and leather, were covered in his signature red flannel. While the look worked on some level, the decor could use a woman's touch.

The reflection led Colt's thoughts to one woman in particular.

"You know who I'm *really* surprised is still single?" Colt broached the question as though they'd never changed the subject.

"Let me guess... Penny?"

Colt chose to ignore Jack's smirk and pressed on. "Why do you think she isn't dating anyone?"

"Beats me. She dated a guy from Primrose Valley a couple of years ago. But it ended after a few months."

An irrational jolt of jealousy shot through him, but Colt quickly squelched it. "What's his story?"

"Some fancy art collector. He seemed nice enough. Bought a painting from her shop, and I guess they hit it off."

"Why do you think it didn't work out?"

Jack paused. Tossing the rag over his shoulder, he leveled his gaze on Colt. "Why do you want to know? Don't tell me you're still interested in Penny."

"Of course not," Colt snorted. "I had a brief moment of insanity when I almost asked her out at the reception. I blame it on the voodoo wedding vibes."

"Are you sure?" Jack frowned, looking unconvinced.

"Look, a relationship would cramp my lifestyle. And besides, she's about as unadventurous as they come. Trust me, I have zero interest in Penny."

Somewhat appeased, Jack returned to his dish towel and damp soda glasses, while Colt's thoughts drifted to the night of Luke's wedding when he and Penny shared a slow, intimate dance.

He'd been surprised by how perfectly she'd fit in his arms. And how easily the conversation flowed. She'd made him feel—

Abruptly, Colt cleared his throat.

Uh-uh... no way....

He would *not* go down that road again.

Dating was out of the question.

Especially Penny Heart—the Queen of Caution.

CHAPTER 6

*H*er heart fluttering, Penny glanced at one of three grandfather clocks in her antiques store, Thistle & Thorn. Colt would darken her doorway any minute to go over their ideas for the top five thrilling adventures in Poppy Creek. She had a feeling he'd disagree with everything on her list, but she planned to stand her ground. And make it unequivocally clear she didn't care what he thought.

So, why had she spent the last hour straightening her shop, making sure each item was displayed in the most appealing arrangement possible before his arrival?

After all, so what if he found her method of organization strange and disorderly? What appeared cluttered and discordant to some had perfect symmetry in her mind. She arranged the shelves based on feeling, instinctively knowing which objects should go where—she never questioned *why*. And she never failed to help a customer find exactly the right treasure, even when they didn't know they were looking for it.

But she had a feeling Colt would take one glance at her hodgepodge store and think she had a screw loose. Or at the very least, that she was a discombobulated mess.

Not that she cared about his opinion.

Brushing her hands together, Penny turned toward her part-time help, Briana Riley. "Are you sure you're fine on your own for a few hours?" she asked, although she needn't have bothered. She had no doubt the recent high school graduate could handle things on her own. Bree had been working at the store on weekends for an entire year, picking up extra hours after graduation to save for college.

Truthfully, Penny couldn't have asked for a more enthusiastic, hardworking employee. Bree planned to major in history and loved being surrounded by antiques and collectibles almost as much as she did.

"Yep! It's been a little slow today, so I think I'll polish the set of Reed & Barton silverware we just got in."

"Perfect! We'll be out back in the garden if you need anything."

As if on cue, Colt waltzed through the front door, the delicate chime of the bell attached to the head jam announcing his entrance. Not that he needed an announcement. With his palpable charisma, Colt Davis was a difficult man to ignore.

But then, so was a bull in a china shop. And in Penny's opinion, both intruders were equally unwelcome.

"Afternoon, ladies! This is quite the place you have here." He nearly stumbled over a stack of steamer trunks propping up an oil landscape painting in a gilded frame.

Bree giggled.

When his gaze fell on the snickering teen, Colt's eyes widened.

Penny almost indulged in a laugh herself, realizing this was the first time Colt had met Bree.

The girl could be considered... a bit eccentric. Rather than wear blue jeans and graphic tees like the rest of her peers, she preferred outfits from different periods in history. Today's ensemble happened to be American colonial—a floral, floor-length gown complete with ruffled sleeves and lace petticoat.

"Uh, excuse me. I forgot how to use my feet for a second." To his credit, Colt righted himself quickly, summoning a heart-stopping grin, the dimple in his left cheek utilized to a dazzling effect. "And you are?"

Blushing profusely, Bree curtsied. "Bri—Briana Riley. I work for Pen—Miss Heart."

Penny covered a smile with the back of her hand. Poor girl. She'd never seen her so flustered. But then, Colt had an uncanny ability to render most women tongue-tied. Emphasis on *most*.

"I'm sure she's lucky to have you. You seem like the kind of person who takes her job seriously."

Still flabbergasted, Bree nodded silently, her round face as pink as the rosebuds dotting her dress. Her huge, doe-like eyes darted to Penny, as though begging for guidance on what to do next.

"She's invaluable," Penny said with genuine warmth. "I don't know what I'll do when she leaves for college in the fall."

"Oh, yeah? Where are you going?" Once again, Colt turned his debilitating smile on Bree, and the color in her cheeks crept into her hairline, contrasting sharply with her fair hair pulled into a taut bun.

"W-Westmont College in Santa Barbara," she stammered.

"Nice place! Near the beach, right?"

Relaxing slightly, Bree flashed a shy smile. "Yes. I can't wait. I've never been to the beach before."

"You'll love it. Surfing. Volleyball. Boogie boarding. Endless fun to be had."

Penny smirked. Of course Colt would list three of the most active beach sports. She imagined he spent countless hours at the ocean during his world travels. With his tanned skin and sun-kissed blond hair, he could be the spokesmodel for Coppertone or Ray-Ban.

"Oh, I probably won't do any of those things." Bree pulled a face. "But I'd like to study under a sun umbrella, listening to the waves. Maybe fly a kite. Oh, and I promised Penny I'd build a sandcastle and send her a photo."

Now it was Penny's turn to blush when Colt shifted his gaze to her crimson face. Why had she asked Bree to build a sandcastle? It seemed silly and childish now. Ridiculous, even. But the request had spilled out of her lips the instant Bree announced her acceptance into Westmont, giddy to be moving so close to the ocean.

Penny dug her nails into her palm, praying Colt didn't press further.

He studied her a moment, his head cocked to one side, before returning his attention to Bree. "That sounds like fun. I'm sure you'll have a great time. And congrats on getting into Westmont. It's a prestigious school. You should be very proud."

"Thanks." Bree dropped her gaze to her vintage leather shoes, but Penny could tell his praise pleased her.

She thought about mentioning how Bree had been offered nearly a full-ride of scholarships, too, but figured the poor girl had been embarrassed enough for one afternoon. "I thought we'd talk in the garden. We can go through the back." Penny gestured for Colt to follow before telling Bree, "Come get me if you need anything."

Colt grinned his goodbye, and Bree wiggled her fingers in a bashful wave.

Clearly, she'd already succumbed to his charm. Penny would have to give her a lecture on the danger of "those kinds of boys" later.

Or really *any* boys, for that matter.

⭐

*H*is pulse quickening in curious anticipation, Colt followed Penny through a heavy brocade curtain into what appeared to be a storage room. Dim and musty, the expansive space burst with an impressive assortment of oddball trinkets ranging from antique typewriters to rusty ice skates to ancient Polaroid cameras.

"This is where we sort through our most recent finds before pricing and displaying them in the store," Penny explained, noticing his awe-stricken expression.

"Does it all come from estate sales?" Colt ran a hand along the mint-condition leather seat of a Schwinn tandem bicycle. It even had the quintessential white wicker basket attached to the handlebars.

"Some of it. I also buy and sell online. But my absolute favorite thing is when people drop items off. Sometimes they'll bring several boxes at a time. It's like Christmas morning. I never know what I'll discover."

Her coppery eyes sparkled from within, and for a moment, Colt found himself captivated, unable to speak for fear his words would somehow whisk away the winsome glow.

Clearing his throat, he asked, "Do you enjoy one particular type of item more than others?"

"As a matter of fact, I do." With an exuberant grin, she skipped toward a long folding table covered in random objects. As though she were revealing a priceless work of art, she held up a black-and-white photograph encased in a dingy wooden frame.

Tilting his head to the side, Colt tried to discern what was so special about the stern, rigid-looking woman in a fur coat gazing at him with a forlorn glint in her coal-black eyes. "Am I missing something?"

Penny flipped the photo facedown. "It's not the image I find fascinating. It's what's *behind* it."

Colt watched, mesmerized by the subtle transformation of

her features, illuminated with wonder, as she removed the backing. "My dad taught me to always check photographs and paintings for an inscription. You won't always find one. And sometimes, when you do, it's merely a scribbled date or location. But if you're *really* lucky, you'll find something special."

"Like what?" Drawn to her infectious energy, Colt stepped closer, peering over her shoulder.

As she peeled the backing away from the photograph, her breath hitched.

But the yellowed paper underneath appeared to be blank.

Or so he thought.

Penny released a tiny squeal of excitement, jabbing her finger at the upper right corner. "There it is!" Squinting, she read the small, looping script out loud. "'My angel. My breath of life. My everything. Elizabeth Rothchild, 1932.' Isn't that the most beautiful thing you've ever seen?" She glanced over her shoulder, their faces so close, he could count the flecks of gold around her irises.

He gulped. Was the inscription the most beautiful thing he'd ever seen?

Not even close….

"Um…" Taking a step back, he ran his fingers through his hair, caught off guard by the thought. "That's pretty cool."

Sighing dreamily, Penny returned her gaze to the faint lettering, nearly faded into nonexistence with the passage of time. "Whenever we found something like this, Dad and I would make up elaborate backstories about the previous owners."

"What would you come up with for this one?" Colt nodded toward the frame still clutched in her hands like a beloved family heirloom.

"Well…" She chewed her bottom lip as she contemplated his question, an adorable self-conscious tick Colt found far too alluring for his own good. "This was taken during the Great Depression. And based on her fur coat, she was probably a woman of means." Her gaze flitted to his face before she quickly glanced away, her cheeks tinged pink.

He expected her to stop, too embarrassed to continue. But she seemed to come alive in the dimly lit, dusty space. Her stunning eyes took on a glazed, faraway look, as though lost in her own thoughts. "Her beau, Gregory Darby, was a poor factory worker without a cent to his name. They had a brief but earth-shattering romance until Elizabeth's father married her off to Archibald Warner, an oil magnate running for political office. Beth gave this photograph to Gregory the night she said goodbye, sealing her farewell with a tender, soul-rending kiss."

Colt stood motionless, completely at a loss for words. The richness of her imagination moved him more than he'd expected. And he doubted any arrangement of letters could adequately encapsulate how he felt. "That's so..." He trailed off, his brain coming up blank. *Imaginative? Romantic? Compelling?* Colt rummaged through his vocabulary, finally blurting, "Sad." He grimaced. Of all the words he could have chosen, he'd gone with *sad? What an idiot.*

Penny flushed, busying herself with returning the backing to its proper position. "Well, despite what Hallmark tries to tell you, most romances end in heartbreak."

Colt couldn't disagree. "Your dad seems like a really neat guy."

"He was." A wistful countenance settled across her features, and she tucked a strand of hair behind her ear, staring at the floor.

"I don't really remember seeing him around town all that often when we were kids," Colt continued. "He must have worked long hours." Truthfully, Timothy Heart was known as quite the odd duck, but he wasn't about to point that out.

"He loved this store. Why would he go anywhere else?"

Her voice carried a faint, defensive quality, so Colt softened his tone. "I can see why. If I were him, I'd have a hard time leaving, too." Now that they were on the subject, Colt realized he'd never heard how her father passed away. "If you don't mind me asking..." he said gently. "What happened to him?"

Her face immediately paled, and Colt could've kicked himself. He, of all people, knew the discomfort caused by supposedly well-meaning questions.

For months after his father's death, barely two seconds went by without someone asking him how he was doing, offering their condolences, or extolling his dad's many virtues.

Leonard Davis had been the town's everyman—always there to lend a hand, no matter what. They'd even begged him to run for mayor, except the position had been held by the Burns men for generations. And Leonard Davis wasn't one to buck tradition. Oh, no. He was as straight as an arrow. Straighter, even. And Luke had turned out just like him. Not that Leonard could say the same for his other son.

Forcing the bitter memories aside, he focused his attention back on Penny. "Hey," he said with a kind smile. "Forget I asked."

Relief flooded her eyes, relaxing the creases around the edges.

"How about we get started on that list?" he offered.

She nodded gratefully, waving for him to follow. "The garden's this way."

Colt kept his gaze trained on her back, observing the gentle swish of her long auburn hair.

He'd always known she was a bit of an enigma.

But now he knew it was more than that.

Penny Heart had a secret.

And probably more than one.

CHAPTER 7

$\mathcal{P}$enny flinched as they stepped from the dimly lit storage room into the brilliant afternoon sunlight. She surreptitiously stole a glance at Colt, gauging his reaction as he took in the intimate garden terrace for the first time.

One half English garden, the other half herbs, fragrant lavender and rosemary stems mingled with delphinium, hollyhocks, and foxglove in a myriad of vibrant colors. Bird baths and feeders dotted the dense foliage, inviting lyrical robins and blue jays to her tiny oasis that abutted the nature trail behind Main Street.

Since she spent almost as much time outside soaking up the tranquil atmosphere, the cozy space felt like an extension of her home. A realization that made her acutely aware of Colt's presence.

He released a low whistle. "Not too shabby." His gaze fell on the white wrought iron bistro table and the rolling beverage cart beside it.

Twenty minutes earlier, she'd set out a pitcher of sweetened jasmine-infused green tea and a covered basket of Eliza's jumbo-size cranberry praline muffins. A tingling warmth crept up her neck.

Was it too much? Did it look like she was trying to impress him? Because she definitely *wasn't*. Setting out snacks was merely the hospitable thing to do.

"Thanks. It's small, but homey." Her sling-back sandals clacked across the stone tiles as she hurried to the table, choosing the chair that faced the back door to keep an eye out for Bree in case she needed something.

Colt plopped onto the chair opposite her, a lazy smile softening his features as he studied the melodic wind chime crafted from an assortment of seashells. "It's so peaceful out here. I could take a nap in *that* for hours." He nodded toward the crocheted hammock swinging invitingly between two dogwood trees, the lush branches creating a shaded canopy overhead.

A vision of his muscular, athletic frame reposed in her favorite reading spot flashed through her mind and she quickly pushed the unwanted—though not entirely unappealing—image aside.

"So, I've already made a list of all five activities." After pouring them each a tall glass of iced tea, she returned the pitcher to the cart and snatched the small leather notebook she'd left there earlier, flipping it open a few pages.

"Let's hear 'em." Colt took a generous sip of iced tea before digging into the basket of muffins.

"First, I have the nature trail."

Colt snorted with laughter before his smile faltered. "Wait. You're serious?"

"Tourists love the nature trail," Penny argued, annoyed she hadn't even made it past the first activity before he uttered his objection.

"Sure, but it's hardly adventurous. Unless you count the time Frida Connelly told everyone she'd seen a mountain lion."

Penny snickered in spite of herself. "And it was only Peggy Sue."

"How she can't tell the difference between a mountain lion and Bill Tucker's pet pig, I'll never know." He shook his head in bemusement. "What else do you have?"

"Well…" Penny glanced at her notes, her confidence wavering. "What about one of Millie's dance classes?"

"I hardly think doing the waltz with a ninety-year-old woman will get your adrenaline pumping."

"What if it's the tango?"

"Maybe," he chuckled. "Is the rest of your list just as death-defying?"

Defensive, Penny jutted her chin a little higher. "It's a perfectly respectable list."

"Sure. *If* you're writing Beverly's original article. You've come up with quite the itinerary for rowdy senior citizens." His intense turquoise-blue eyes twinkled with humor, and for a moment, Penny forgot to be outraged.

But only for a moment.

"I'm sorry you find it so boring," she said stiffly. "If you want to quit, I completely understand."

"I'm not going to quit. But what about my ideas? I thought we were a team." Colt flashed his dimple, rattling her resolve.

"Technically, this was my assignment first. Which means my vote should count for more than yours."

"But Burns made me your partner specifically for my expertise. We both know he'll never approve your list. C'mon. Just take a tiny peek at mine." He leaned forward, pinning her with his most persuasive smile. "Besides, the sooner Burns approves the list, the sooner we can get it over with. You *do* want to get it over with, don't you? Unless you're secretly looking forward to spending time with me."

Her spine rigid, she thrust out her hand. "Let me see it."

Grinning, Colt reached into his back pocket and retrieved a single sheet of paper folded in fours and crumpled beyond belief.

Penny rolled her eyes as she yanked it from his grasp. Smoothing it out on the table, she scanned his chicken scratch, her eyes widening in horror. Shoving the paper toward him, she shook her head. "There's no way I'm doing anything on that list."

"C'mon. You barely looked at it," he cajoled, sliding it back toward her.

She folded her arms in front of her chest. "Nothing in the world could convince me to do any of those things."

"Not even Beverly?"

Seething, she narrowed her eyes into slits. That was a low blow. Mostly because he was right. She couldn't go back on her promise to Beverly. Even if Mayor Burns *had* changed everything at the last minute.

"Here. I'll make a compromise," Colt offered, grabbing her notebook.

"What kind of compromise?"

"I'll add one of your ideas to my list." He trailed his finger down the page, pausing halfway toward the bottom. "Here. This could work. It's completely different from the activities I chose, but it's thrilling in its own way. And I'm kind of partial to the culinary angle." Plucking the pen resting in the spine, he scratched out the last item on his list and added hers. "Perfect. It's all settled." Refolding the sheet of paper, he stuffed it back inside his pocket before helping himself to another muffin.

Dumbfounded, Penny stared as he tore off a sizable chunk and tossed it to a pair of sparrows scrounging the ground for insects. Colt smiled to himself as they eagerly gobbled up the scattered crumbs.

She blinked at the unexpectedly warmhearted gesture.

Finishing the baked good, Colt rose, beaming down at her. "I'll run the list by Burns before I head back to Frank's. I'll be by to pick you up tomorrow morning."

"What time?"

"I'll be here at eight o'clock sharp. With spurs on." To her chagrin, he actually winked. "See you then, partner."

Glowering, she resisted the urge to protest. Arguing with Colt was obviously futile. So much for standing her ground.

The first activity flashed in her mind, and she nearly choked on the lump of anxiety lodged in her throat. Hastily, she downed half her glass of iced tea in one gulp.

There was no way she'd survive the list.

Or spending time with Colt.

☆

On the ride back to Frank's, Colt couldn't get the flicker of panic in Penny's eyes out of his mind. She'd looked genuinely terrified by his proposed activities.

At the wedding, she'd mentioned having a long list of phobias, but he'd assumed she'd been joking. Or at the very least, exaggerating.

But now… he wasn't so sure.

What kind of person didn't enjoy a little fun and excitement? Try as he might, he couldn't figure her out. One moment, she exuded this captivating energy. The next, she seemed to recoil into a tight, convoluted knot of fear.

And to his surprise, he wanted to help untangle it.

Warm wind whipped past him as he zipped around another bend in the winding mountain road. He loved the freedom of his motorcycle—the sensation of the air curving around his body, inviting him to push the limits even further.

He knew he sounded cliché, but living on the edge made him feel alive. Plus, it meant honoring his father's dying wish—words he'd never shared with anyone. Not even Luke.

At the memory of his father, his chest constricted, making the snug fit of his padded motorcycle jacket close to unbearable.

Skidding to a stop in the gravel driveway, Colt yanked off his helmet, gasping for air as though he'd been suffocating.

Spotting Beverly's Volvo in the covered parking stall, he decided to slip around the side of the house and use the back entrance so he wouldn't disturb them.

Arriving at his room, Colt carefully turned the door handle, slowly nudging it open to avoid the betraying squeak of the hinges. After quietly clicking the latch shut, he shrugged out of his jacket and draped it across an ironing board that doubled as a table. Since Frank didn't have proper guest accommodations, Cassie had fixed up what appeared to be a storage space, situating a twin mattress in between stacks of cardboard boxes filled with copies of Frank's first book, *The Mariposa Method*—waiting to be signed, he assumed—and even more boxes bursting with fan mail rerouted by his publisher.

Every single envelope remained unopened. Apparently, Frank didn't write for accolades. Not that Colt was surprised. After all, the man had used a pseudonym so he could maintain his reclusive lifestyle. Until Cassie came knocking on his door last Christmas and turned Frank's life upside down.

Colt smiled to himself at the musing. His sister-in-law sure was a force of nature. Since meeting her, even ever-dependable Luke had changed professions, giving up their father's law practice. A revelation Colt still found unsettling.

Kicking off his boots, he flopped onto the bed, landing on something sharp and solid.

Groaning, he plucked a hardback edition of Frank's book from its uncomfortable position lodged in his side.

Noticing the Post-it note stuck to the glossy cover, he ripped it off with one quick yank before squinting at the cursive script.

Finish this by Monday morning. Then the real work begins.

Crumpling the note, Colt closed his eyes with a heavy sigh.

Great... he'd almost forgotten about this part of the arrangement.

Normally, he wasn't a fan of manual labor. He preferred to pay his meager bills with more engaging jobs like exotic car salesman and skydiving instructor.

But he also knew the importance of having a purpose in life—a passion—particularly for someone in Frank's position.

Besides, how hard could it be?

CHAPTER 8

*G*runting, Colt shoved the heavy book off his chest, struggling to sit upright in bed. He'd fallen asleep in the worst possible position and now had a huge kink in his neck to show for it. But once he'd started reading *The Mariposa Method*, he couldn't put it down. He'd been gripped by the opening paragraph, which recounted Frank's first visit to a coffee plantation in Colombia. The vivid depiction of his confrontation with a gun runner for the drug cartel bent on controlling local farmers by brute force had Colt pinned to the page.

The remainder of the book chronicled Frank's riveting journey from coffee enthusiast to world-renowned roaster. Developing his unique coffee roasting process had been a tumultuous labor of love fraught with heart-wrenching highs and lows. And Colt developed a newfound respect for the cantankerous inventor. But more than that, the passionate, almost tender language Frank used to describe the process stirred something in Colt... an intense curiosity to witness the artistry he so colorfully described. If he wasn't looking forward to the day's adventure, he'd wish it was already Monday.

Another unexpected outcome of finishing Frank's book was

how badly he craved a rich, flavorful cup of coffee. In fact, he doubted he'd ever view the caffeinated beverage in quite the same way again. Through Frank's powerful prose, coffee roasting had sparked a similar allure as one of Colt's favorite hobbies— cooking. He admired the way a skilled chef could transform the simplest ingredient from mere sustenance into an unforgettable experience. With Frank's groundbreaking method, even a lowly robusta bean could tantalize the taste buds of the most refined palate. If *that* wasn't culinary magic, Colt didn't know what was.

Quickly dressing in dark denim jeans and his favorite cotton T-shirt, he padded down the hallway into the kitchen. Halfway there, he detected the heady aroma of a fresh pot of coffee. If he remembered correctly from his late-night reading, the nutty undertones meant Frank had brewed a Colombian bean.

Entering the modest kitchen, Colt spotted Frank at the counter muttering under his breath as he tried to operate a hand crank grinder while leaning on his walker. *Yeesh.* Keeping Frank off his feet would be harder than he thought if the man kept waking up at the crack of dawn. Not to mention he seemed incapable of actually *asking* for help.

"Need a hand?" Noting the prepped French press, Colt realized the smell he'd attributed to brewed coffee actually emanated from the grounds.

"Why not? Make yourself useful." Abandoning the grinder, Frank hobbled to the kitchen table, sinking into one of the mismatched chairs with a labored grunt. "I need two more tablespoons."

"I'm on it." Colt grabbed the antique grinder, curling his fingers around the cool, gold-plated metal etched with elaborate carvings. It reminded him of a fancy pepper mill; it had the same cylindrical shape, topped with a hand crank. Based on the aged patina, it had been in Frank's family for generations. "Is this an heirloom?"

The old man tipped his head in a noncommittal nod.

"Let me guess..." Colt continued, turning the crank. The beans crunched inside the contraption, releasing the same intoxicating scent he'd smelled earlier. "It belonged to your mother?" Frank had mentioned she was Armenian, and the intricate pattern definitely had a Middle Eastern influence.

"If I wanted to be interviewed, I would have said yes to Kelly Ripa," Frank grumbled. "She's easier on the eyes."

"Fair enough," Colt chuckled, adding two scoops to the glass carafe before securing the stainless-steel lid and plunger.

Clearly, his ill-humored host would be a tough nut to crack.

Cassie had assured him Frank wasn't usually this cranky, blaming his gruff demeanor on his poor health and limitations. Colt tried to be understanding, but Frank still seemed to give him a harder time than anyone else. Which struck him as odd. It seemed unlikely Frank harbored a grudge from Colt's trespassing days in high school. So, where did the enormous chip on his shoulder come from?

"Have any plans for the day?" Colt asked. He already knew Cassie was coming by to work on the book they were writing together—a second edition of *The Mariposa Method*—but he'd hoped to make conversation while they waited for the coffee to steep. Otherwise, it would be the longest four minutes of his life.

"You mean besides climbing Mount Kilimanjaro?"

The sarcastic inflection wasn't lost on Colt, and he gritted his teeth. Every pass he threw, Frank deflected. Just once, could they be on the same team? "I hope you'll be back in time for shish kebab tonight. I plan on firing up the grill around six o'clock."

Colt had prepared way more than they needed so they'd have extra for the coming weeks. Tonight's skewers were prepped and waiting in the refrigerator along with a tray of hand-rolled grape leaves and a big bowl of tabbouleh—a special salad comprised primarily of fresh parsley harvested from his mother's garden.

Confident he'd outdone himself, Colt couldn't wait to see the look on Frank's face when he arranged everything on the table.

He'd even talked Eliza into baking some pita bread to pair with his homemade hummus. Top it all off with the buttery pilaf Frank requested, and not even the King of Crabbiness could maintain a foul mood when faced with such a feast. Especially when he saw the box of baklava Colt ordered from a specialty shop in San Francisco for dessert.

"I'll be here," Frank mumbled. Although he wasn't exactly smiling, the hard lines around his eyes had softened.

While far from a touchdown, Colt had at least crossed the twenty-yard line.

He could only hope the same luck carried into his afternoon with Penny.

*A*s Penny stood on the sidewalk waiting for Colt, she fidgeted with the nickel-plated belt buckle cinching her vintage Levi's. Maybe she'd gone a bit overboard in preparation for the day's activity. But she'd hoped the bright teal cowboy boots and soft chambray button-down tied at the waist would instill some confidence. If she couldn't play the part, she could at least *look* it.

The rumble of Colt's motorcycle in the distance matched the growl of her stomach. A jumble of nerves, she hadn't been able to eat breakfast, settling for a cup of ginger tea with a teaspoon of orange blossom honey. While the day's activity wasn't the most outrageous item on Colt's list, she still found the prospect daunting.

Colt eased into a parking spot in front of Thistle & Thorn and planted his feet on the ground to balance the heavy bike. Catching sight of her on the curb, he flipped up his visor, staring slack-jawed.

Apparently, he approved of her outfit choice.

Heat swept across her collarbone, climbing all the way up her neck. For some unknown reason, his appreciative gaze sent tingles shooting down her spine. *Stop it, stop it*, she chided her traitorous hormones.

Penny almost didn't hear his throat clear over the hum of the engine. Or was it her thundering heartbeat?

"Ready?" He removed a spare helmet from the cargo net before offering it to her.

She took a step back. "You've lost your mind if you think I'm getting on that thing."

"C'mon," he coaxed with a teasing lilt. "It's fun. You might enjoy it."

"You know what I *really* enjoy? Being alive."

He released a rich, hearty laugh, clearly not taking her seriously.

Planting one hand on her hip, she raised both eyebrows. "Did you know motorcycles are twenty-seven percent more dangerous than driving a car?"

He merely shrugged, flashing his boyish grin again.

"Well, if *you* want to become an accident report, be my guest," she huffed. "But I'm driving." Digging inside her purse, she pulled out the key to her 1965 Ford Mustang.

She hid a smug smile as Colt killed his engine the second she popped opened the driver's door.

"She's yours?" He didn't bother hiding his shock as he hopped off his bike, removing his helmet to get a better look.

"My dad and I restored her together." She tossed her purse in the back seat before sliding onto the silky black upholstery.

"She's a beaut." Colt whistled, running his hand along the flawless paint job—a satiny cream color that reminded Penny of a pristine white sand beach.

"Thanks. It took us almost a decade to restore her former glory."

"So, everything's original?" Colt popped open the passenger door and climbed inside.

"Pretty much," she said proudly.

His gaze landed on the state-of-the-art seat belts, and she flushed. "Well, except for those." Yanking on the shoulder strap, she clicked hers in place before taking a few moments to triple-check her mirrors.

Colt stared at her as though she were an old fuddy-duddy, but she didn't care. Better safe than sorry.

"What about air conditioning?" he asked, eyeing the dashboard.

"It's called fresh air." She leaned across him to manually roll down his window. *Big mistake.* Her stomach fluttered as she caught a whiff of his body wash—crisp and exhilarating like a cool ocean breeze. She scrambled back to her side of the car as quickly as possible, mentally chastising herself again.

Okay, so she wasn't completely immune to his outward appeal. But that's all it was—a pleasant exterior, like quicksand disguised as a scenic beach. If she got too close, disaster would surely strike.

"You can find a radio station, if you want," she told him, desperate for a distraction.

"What kind of music do you like?"

"Anything. I'm not picky." She avoided making eye contact as she glanced over her shoulder to back out of the parking space.

But an unexpected movement darted across her peripheral vision and she slammed on the brakes, lurching them forward. "What are you doing?" she snapped, grabbing the back of her neck. "Did you drop something down my shirt?" In a panic, she jammed her hand down her collar, praying she wouldn't find a centipede again. Or worse—a spider.

"Relax. You had a leaf in your braid." Colt pinched the offending foliage between his fingers, eyeing her like she'd lost her mind.

"Oh." She smiled sheepishly before puckering her lips in a defensive pout. "Although, it's not like you can blame me for expecting the worst. My collar has been the gateway for insects, ice cubes, and itching powder, thanks to you."

Now it was Colt's turn to grin sheepishly. "You're right. And I'm sorry about that."

Penny blinked. Did Colt just apologize? *No*... she must be imagining things. Before she could confirm her delusion, Bree burst out of the shop, nearly tripping over the hem of her Renaissance-era gown. "Are you okay? You hit the brakes pretty hard."

Embarrassed, Penny slouched in her seat, just shy of sinking into the footwell as she offered a feeble flap of her wrist. "We're fine. Nothing to worry about."

Relief flickered across Bree's face as she gathered the sapphire-velvet folds of her dress in one hand, while waving with the other. "Oh, good. You guys have fun!"

"We will!" Colt shouted out the window cheerfully.

Penny forced a smile, biting back a cynical quip as she pulled onto Main Street.

The day would be anything *but* fun.

As if mocking her plight, the speakers crackled and the high-pitched harmony of the Beach Boys' "Don't Worry Baby" filled the space between them.

Colt bobbed his head in approval. "Now *this* is perfect driving music."

To her chagrin, he proceeded to bellow the chorus with uninhibited gusto.

She suppressed a groan.

Based on the events ahead—not to mention the company— she had every reason to worry.

CHAPTER 9

*T*o her immense surprise, prickles of excitement skittered up Penny's spine as they stood outside the stables of Lupine Ridge Ranch waiting to saddle up.

Saddle up. She'd expected the prospect to fill her with dread, but she found herself brimming with unprecedented anticipation.

Maybe it had something to do with the intoxicating aroma of rich soil, sweet-smelling hay bales, and invigorating pine trees. Or the gorgeous, Pinterest-worthy property—acres of lush meadows, an exquisite two-story lodge, and a long row of elegant stables nestled beside a peaceful brook.

Whatever the reason, she'd never experienced this kind of exhilaration before. And she didn't hate it.

To think, she'd almost nixed the idea. Partly because she'd wanted to dismiss everything on Colt's list. Plus, the ranch technically sat halfway across the county line, making it a part of Poppy Creek *and* their sister town, Lupine Ridge. But since Burns had approved it, Colt wouldn't let her back out. And while she hated to admit it, she admired his persistence.

As Penny snuck a glance in his direction, she caught him watching her.

"Excited?" His lips twitched, and Penny could sense an *I told you so* coming on.

She shrugged, playing it cool. "A little, maybe."

"I thought you hated horses." He leaned against the split-rail fence, his playful gaze holding hers.

"No. I hate snakes, piranhas, poisonous spiders, and confrontational kangaroos. Horses are fine. It's being thrown *off* them I don't particularly care for."

Colt chuckled. "If it helps, we can request their shortest one. You know, to decrease the distance between you and the ground."

"Gee, thanks." Penny rolled her eyes but couldn't help a smile. Not even Colt's childishness could ruin her good mood.

She opened her mouth to make a sarcastic retort, but her words faltered as a tall, distractingly handsome man approached them from the stables. In his plaid shirt and fitted Wrangler jeans, he could star in a Stetson cologne commercial.

Colt noticed her flabbergasted expression and turned to follow her gaze.

A slow, friendly smile stretched across the man's rugged, chiseled features. "You must be Colt and Penny. Welcome to the ranch. What do you think of it so far?"

"It's breathtaking." Penny found it difficult to tear her gaze from his gentle, honest eyes. Behind thick lashes, they shimmered a deep amber color that reminded her of black Darjeeling tea.

"Thank you kindly. I can't take too much credit, though. It looked like this when I bought it."

He exuded a genuine, humble warmth Penny found instantly appealing. And for a fleeting moment, she lamented her no-dating policy.

"You own this place?" Colt asked with a scrutinizing stare.

"Shoot. Where are my manners? I'm Hunter. Hunter West."

He offered his hand to Colt, who shook it reluctantly. "I bought the ranch a few years back from the original owner, Gus Walker. Are you two from around here?"

"We're from the next town over."

Penny didn't want to read into anything, but the way Colt said *we* almost made it sound like they were a couple. And for some reason, she felt the need to clarify. "I live in Poppy Creek, where I run an antiques store. Colt's visiting family for the summer. We're actually writing an article on adventurous activities in the area for our town's guidebook."

"Well, you've come to the right place," Hunter drawled with an effortless smile. "Have you been horseback riding before?"

"No, I haven't," Penny admitted.

"Then I'll make sure you get my favorite mount." He flashed his perfect teeth again. "Wait here. I'll be back in two shakes of a lamb's tail."

Less than thirty seconds after Hunter left, Colt muttered, "Talk about unprofessional."

"What do you mean? I thought he was perfectly professional."

"Of course you did," Colt snorted. "He's flirting with you."

"He is not," she insisted, suddenly flustered.

"It's as plain as the blush on your face."

"Don't be ridiculous." Penny glanced away, uncomfortable with the dark glint in Colt's eyes—almost as though he were jealous. But that would be crazy. Even if Hunter *was* flirting—which he most certainly wasn't—why would Colt care?

Unsettled by the thought, Penny straightened as Hunter emerged from the stables leading two of the most beautiful horses she'd ever seen.

"Here ya go. Maverick is your ride today." He passed the tawny leather reins to Colt.

"Well, aren't you a nice-looking fellow?" Colt crooned, softening slightly as he pet the horse's glossy black coat. "Named after Tom Cruise in *Top Gun*, by any chance?"

"Sure is." Hunter grinned. "I noticed the airplane emblem on your T-shirt and figured you two would get along. Do you fly?"

"Yeah. I took my first solo in a Cessna 172 about five years ago. You?"

"I've been around planes since before I could walk. I fly a Piper Super Cub. There's a landing strip on the ranch if you want to go up sometime."

Penny hid a smirk at the conflicted crease in Colt's forehead. She could tell he wanted to find fault with Hunter, but the man was making it difficult.

"Thanks. I just might." Colt rubbed Maverick's neck as though they'd been pals for years.

"And for you,"—Hunter said, turning toward Penny—"I have Frost."

"As in Robert Frost? He's my favorite poet."

"Aw, shucks. I'm tempted to say yes. But he's actually named Frost because he's a Camarillo White Horse. They're incredibly rare. Somehow, I had a feeling you'd appreciate that."

Flushing all the way to the tips of her ears, Penny buried her face in the horse's alabaster mane. "He's gorgeous."

"And a gentle ride for first-timers. Did you guys sign up for a tour? I'd be happy to take you."

"We're doing the self-guided tour," Colt said with a firm note of finality. "But thanks."

"Some other time, then." Hunter tipped his wide-brimmed cowboy hat in casual acknowledgment. "There are several great trails. The one that leads to Lake Chickadee is my favorite."

"Thanks. We'll check it out." Colt seemed eager to escape, and Penny shot him a reproachful glare before turning a grateful smile on Hunter.

"Thank you so much for all your help."

"Anytime." He shuffled his feet shyly before adding, "I'm always looking for interesting items to decorate the lodge. I'll have to look up your place in Poppy Creek and swing by some time."

"I'd like that." The words slipped out before she had time to think, and she immediately regretted them. She didn't want to lead him on. He seemed like a great guy. And it wasn't personal. She'd turn down Prince Charming himself if he showed up at her door with a glass slipper and empty promises.

To her relief, Maverick whinnied and stomped his feet, as though he'd had enough of their small talk.

Hunter's gaze lingered on her a moment longer before he stepped back, waving goodbye. "Enjoy your ride."

"Thanks, I'm sure I will."

As she reached up to stroke Frost's mane, she realized her anxiety had completely melted away, as if the horse had magical soothing powers.

She only hoped the spell would last.

⭐

"*G*ood job, buddy. I knew you were on my side," Colt whispered into Maverick's ear as the stallion clomped along the trail a few feet behind Penny and Frost.

As soon as the horse had whinnied, interrupting Hunter's obnoxious—and way too obvious—flirting, Colt felt an irrational bond with his new equine friend. Apparently, horses *could* sense human emotion. And Colt's agitation had spoken volumes to the sympathetic stallion. Not that anyone could blame him for being irritated. Hunter had a lot of nerve hitting on Penny right in front of him. For all he knew, they were a couple.

Fueled by his frustration, Colt muttered, "What kind of name is Hunter, anyway?"

"What do you mean? It's a pretty common name," Penny responded over the rhythmic *clip-clop* of Frost's hooves on the dirt trail.

"But Hunter West? For a guy who owns a dude ranch? C'mon, it's clearly made up."

Penny laughed. "Says the guy who's literally named after a horse. A baby horse, to be exact."

"Touché, Penelope Pitstop." Colt cracked a teasing grin.

"Hey!" Penny twisted in the saddle to glare at him, although the shimmer in her coppery eyes belied her tone. "I am *not* named after the Hanna-Barbera cartoon character."

"My apologies, Punky Brewster."

Her eyes narrowed further, although her lips curled at the edges. "I'm not named after *that* Penelope, either."

"Don't tell me…." Colt furrowed his brow in thought, loving the way she smirked, daring him to guess. "You're the faithful wife of Odysseus from Homer's *Odyssey*."

Her eyes widened. "How did you know?"

"A striking beauty with many suitors? Let's just say the name fits."

She whipped her head forward, but not before Colt noticed the pink tint to her cheeks. "I don't have *any* suitors, let alone many."

"You have at least one," he teased, realizing *two* might be more accurate.

For some reason, in this new environment, he'd started to see Penny in a completely different light.

And the thought of spending more time with her wasn't entirely unpleasant.

"Not Hunter again," she groaned.

"'The lady doth protest too much, methinks.'"

"You're incorrigible," she mumbled. But even though he could no longer see her face, Colt heard her smile.

"When did you start going by Penny?"

"Since I was little. Although, my dad always called me Sweet P."

Her voice softened at the admission, and she leaned forward

to caress Frost's mane.

Colt rolled the moniker over in his mind, appreciating the sound of it. "I like it. And I seem to recall coming up with my own nickname for you in third grade."

Her laughter mingled with the twittering of songbirds in the branches overhead. "Don't remind me!"

"What? You didn't like Pepper? I thought it was kind of cute. You know, like a chili pepper. Because of your red hair."

"Oh, I get it. I just didn't like it. But it makes perfect sense now," she giggled.

Curious, Colt cocked his head. "Meaning?"

"Meaning... you and spicy food don't get along." Tossing him an impish grin, she tapped Frost with her heels, and the horse gladly broke into a trot.

Chuckling to himself, Colt relaxed in the saddle, fully enjoying their playful banter. In fact, the afternoon was turning out to be one for the record books. He and Penny Heart... actually getting along.

Savoring the tranquility of the surrounding forest, he filled his lungs with the crisp, woodsy scent of pine sap and cedar, marveling at how comfortable and at ease Penny looked, her thick braid bouncing against her back with each graceful undulation of her body.

A quiet satisfaction stole over him, solidifying in his heart that horseback riding had been the right choice for their first adventure.

"How's it going up there, fearless leader?" he asked, hoping she'd confirm his supposition.

"Great! Frost seems to know exactly where he's going." Glancing over her shoulder, Penny gifted him with the most joyful smile he'd ever seen. The way streaks of sunlight broke through the branches and danced across her face momentarily stole his breath. It sounded cheesy, even inside his own head, but she looked like a perfect summer day personified.

And he never wanted it to end.

No sooner than the thought had crossed his mind, Frost froze in his tracks, nostrils flaring.

"What is it, boy?" Penny purred, leaning forward to pat his neck.

The horse's ears shot back as he released a high-pitched whinny.

"What's wrong?" Colt pulled on the reins, coming to a stop behind her.

"I don't know. It's like he—"

A telltale rattle cut her sentence short, and her entire body stiffened.

"C-Colt?" Her wide, panicked eyes never left the rattlesnake squirming in the center of their path.

"Try to stay calm. Everything will be fine." Keeping his tone low and steady, Colt racked his brain for a solution. Maybe if they ignored it, the critter would leave on its own?

"This isn't real… this isn't real…." Penny whispered some sort of mantra, her fear evident in the shakiness of her breath.

Colt tightened his grip. He had to do something—*anything*. But what? Prepared to hop off Maverick and face the surly serpent mano a mano, he lost the chance when it darted toward Frost.

The terrified horse reared on his hind legs before vaulting over his attacker, tearing down the trail as though the snake were hot on his hooves.

Penny's piercing scream echoed in the cloud of dust left behind.

A cold dread gripped Colt's chest as he pressed his heels into Maverick's side, urging him to follow.

As they galloped through the forest, Colt's eyes burned as he stared into the wind, determined to keep Penny in his sights. Towering trees closed in around them, whipping his arms and legs with spindly branches, finally relenting when they broke through the other side, revealing a picturesque lake surrounded by sloping, sandy banks.

Colt would have been impressed with the breadth of the body of water if he weren't worried that Penny seemed to be headed straight for it. "Pull back on the reins!"

Understandably, she appeared more concerned with holding on for dear life than navigating.

"C'mon, Mav. You've got this," he encouraged the steed. If only they could catch up, he might have a shot at stopping Frost before he charged into the lake.

Maverick valiantly gave it his all; the sinewy muscles in his haunches flexed with exertion. But Frost—the snow-white fury— was faster.

His pulse racing, Colt watched helplessly as the crazed horse sprinted toward the water's edge. But as soon as his hooves made contact, he lurched to a stop, launching Penny out of the saddle like a Hail Mary pass.

At her petrified scream, Colt's heart leapt into his throat. Did she know how to swim? Not waiting to find out, he yanked on the reins, bringing Maverick to an abrupt halt.

Springing to the ground, Colt dove headfirst into the icy water, summoning his most powerful breaststroke to reach Penny as quickly as possible. Acting on instinct, he looped one arm around her waist and towed her back to shore.

Sputtering and gasping for breath, Penny lay facedown in the sand, her sopping-wet clothes clinging to her shivering body.

"Are you okay?" As Colt watched her shoulders shake, a protective urge to wrap her in his arms washed over him.

This was his fault. He'd hoped to assuage her fears and show her a good time, not traumatize her to death. How could he fix this?

Tentatively, he laid a hand on her quaking shoulder. "Pen?"

To his shock, Penny rolled onto her back, giggling uncontrollably. "See! *That's* why I hate snakes." Breathless from laughing so hard, she gazed up at him, her cheeks flushed, her eyes bright and glimmering.

Suddenly, Colt felt an overwhelming urge to cup her face in his hands and kiss her—right then and there.

He'd seen plenty of beautiful women before. Literally tens of thousands, from all around the world.

But Penny? She topped them all.

There was something about her—a vibrant, infectious light that radiated from deep within her soul, illuminating her entire being.

Not to mention she was full of surprises.

He'd expected her to be upset, maybe even angry. Not laugh it off.

Boy, did he have a lot to learn about this woman.

And as he gazed into her laughter-filled eyes, he realized he desperately wanted to know everything.

Even if it meant sticking around town for a lot longer than he'd planned.

CHAPTER 10

*T*he entire ride back to Frank's, Colt wrestled with a knot of guilt in the pit of his stomach. He'd had an incredible afternoon—the kind that left a lasting impression.

But it had come at a cost.

And when he'd called to tell Luke he wouldn't make it back in time to grill the shish kebabs, his brother's disappointed silence had spoken volumes.

To make matters worse, Luke didn't seem all that surprised.

As Colt slowed to a stop in the driveway, the knot twisted even tighter when Luke and Cassie emerged through the front door illuminated by the porch light.

Catching sight of Colt, Luke paused and murmured something in Cassie's ear. She nodded slowly and after flashing Colt a small, sympathetic smile, proceeded to the pickup truck on her own.

Luke waited at the bottom of the steps, arms crossed in front of his chest. His sober expression didn't bode well.

Colt ripped off his helmet. "I know, I know. You don't have to say it." He swung his leg over the bike, cringing at the uncomfortable friction of his wet jeans.

"What happened?" Luke eyed his damp T-shirt as Colt unzipped his motorcycle jacket.

"Look, it wasn't my fault." He'd rehearsed a lengthy explanation, but his excuse faltered as Luke's features crumbled.

Releasing a heavy sigh, his brother ran a hand through his hair—dark and wavy, like their mother's. Colt always found it ironic that he'd inherited his father's looks instead of Luke, boasting the same golden-blond hair and turquoise-blue eyes. Although, apparently, he wasn't endowed with any of his superior character traits.

"Listen, Colt…"

Uh-oh… here it comes…. Colt sucked in a breath, ready for the lecture.

Luke's voice softened. "If you can't handle this, let me know. We'll find someone else."

Colt winced at the quiet resignation laced in his brother's words. Clearly, the question was rhetorical. Luke didn't believe he could handle it. And so far, Colt hadn't given him much reason to think otherwise.

"It won't happen again." With unwavering focus, Colt met his brother's gaze.

Luke studied him a moment before murmuring, "I hope not." He took a step toward the truck, then paused to add, "Frank already ate. We brought him dinner from Jack's. He's in the den watching reruns of *The Andy Griffith Show*. He should be fine for a while. Just check on him before you turn in for the night, okay?"

"Got it." Reading between the lines, Colt took the hint that Frank wasn't in the mood for company. Especially not his. Not that he could blame him.

"Well, good night." Luke dipped his head in a half-hearted farewell before hopping in the driver's seat.

Colt followed their taillights until they disappeared from sight before dragging his gaze to the front door. Rationally, he knew the delay was outside his control. But somehow, he still felt responsible. Or rather, *irresponsible.*

Inhaling a fortifying breath, Colt trudged up the porch steps. As he pushed through the front door, he was bombarded by the loud blare of the TV. Frank didn't even notice as he strode past the den, heading straight for his room to change. Forgoing a hot shower, he stripped out of his wet clothes and into basketball shorts and a soft cotton T-shirt.

Slipping into the kitchen for a quick bite to eat, he tore the wrapper off a protein bar and tossed it in the trash. A takeout container rested on a mound of coffee grounds and a rotting banana peel. Out of curiosity, he glanced at the receipt taped to the top—*1 barbecue chicken salad. No dressing. No bacon. No cheese.*

He grimaced. How unpalatable. In his opinion, one of the worst side effects of any illness was the bland food.

Suddenly inspired, Colt ducked into the pantry. Shoving aside a large sack of Samuel Ball's Snow White Flour, he grabbed the box of baklava he'd hidden there earlier in anticipation of the Armenian feast.

After tearing open the package, he arranged several of the honey-soaked treats on a plate before nestling it on a wooden serving tray. Next, he set about grinding fresh coffee beans, being careful to mix in decaf to moderate the caffeine.

Using Frank's antique grinder, Colt adjusted the setting to produce a silky-fine powder. After scooping the ground coffee and a teaspoon of sugar into the *surjep*—an Armenian coffeepot with a copper bottom and narrow pouring spout—Colt added water and set it on the stove.

As the mixture warmed over low heat, Colt grabbed two small demitasse cups and plopped a couple of cardamom seeds in the bottom of each one. Then, for the next few minutes, he kept a watchful eye on the coffee concoction, removing it from the heat for a few seconds whenever it came close to the boiling point.

He'd observed both Frank and Cassie go through the steps of

making Armenian coffee several times, but never realized how therapeutic the process could be. Something about the balance of technical accuracy and intuition soothed his troubled thoughts.

Gripping the long wooden handle, Colt shut off the burner and slowly poured the syrupy liquid into the cups, savoring the rich, spicy aroma as the steam curled toward him in delicate wisps.

Lastly, he scooped the thick foam evenly between the two servings. Placing the tiny cups beside the baklava, he hoisted the tray, praying Frank would accept his peace offering.

From his position in the recliner, Frank eyed Colt suspiciously as he entered the den. His expression remained stoic, but Colt caught the subtle flicker of interest as Frank sniffed the air, recognizing the familiar aroma.

Colt slid the tray onto the coffee table, then straightened, squaring his shoulders. "Frank, I realize I screwed up tonight. I gave you my word, and then I didn't follow through. For that, I'm sorry."

His pulse throbbing in his ears, Colt waited for Frank's response.

And waited.

He shifted his feet, squirming under the weight of the old man's scrutinizing gaze.

Finally, Frank muttered, "I already brushed my teeth."

Releasing the breath he'd been holding, Colt grinned. "Then it's time to be a rebel. What do you say?"

A brief flicker of hesitation flashed across Frank's withered features. Then, to Colt's surprise, he cracked a faint smile. "Don't tell the womenfolk."

"I wouldn't dream of it." After passing him one of the tiny cups and the plate of baklava, Colt settled into the plush corner of the couch, stealing a glimpse of Frank in his peripheral vision.

He noticed his hunched shoulders relax, and the subtle curl to his lips as he sampled his first sip, offering unspoken approval with the micro expression.

As they watched the show in companionable silence, Colt's thoughts drifted to his father, recalling all the evenings they'd spent laughing over the antics of Andy Griffith and his comical deputy, Barney.

At the end of every show, Colt, Luke, and their father would discuss the episode's moral lesson. As a child, he hadn't always appreciated his dad's steady source of wisdom and guidance. But now, more than anything, Colt wanted to ask him for advice.

Mainly, on how he could keep the promise he'd made him….

And pursue Penny Heart.

"*Hi*, Chip! I'm home." Penny's singsong voice cut through the silence of her apartment.

Chip slipped from his warming rock beneath the heat lamp and scooted across the carpet to greet her.

"Did you miss me?" She dumped her purse and the plastic bag containing her wet clothing on the kitchen counter.

Even an hour after her death-defying adventure, her pulse raced with exhilaration, making the ground beneath her feet feel lighter than air. She imagined the sensation would rival standing on the edge of the ocean for the first time, her toes in the water, her gaze set on the horizon, soaking up the endless expanse.

Squatting on the floor, she nuzzled the top of Chip's head with the tip of her finger. "You should have seen me today. I was thrown from a horse into the lake. And you know what? I found it rather thrilling."

His eyelids narrowed into skeptical slits.

"I can hardly believe it myself," she said with a laugh.

Clambering to her feet, she straightened the hem of the denim shirt dress Hunter gave her from the gift shop. Her lips stretched into an involuntary smile as she smoothed the front pocket emblazoned with the ranch's logo. It had been so sweet of him to provide her with a change of clothes. He'd extended the offer to Colt, as well. But he'd stubbornly refused.

Penny shook her head, bemused by the memory. The entire drive home, Colt had insisted he didn't mind staying wrapped in a towel, marinating in his soggy jeans and T-shirt. But his entire body had to be one big prune by now.

She grinned at the thought, then jumped, startled by a knock at the door.

"It's open!" Leaning against the counter, she slipped out of her boots.

Fortunately, when Frost launched her from the saddle, she'd flown right out of her shoes, which had remained tangled in the stirrups.

"What happened? Tell me everything!" Eliza burst through the front door, cradling a large pastry box from the café.

Cassie followed close at her heels.

"What do you mean?" Penny asked, amused by Eliza's breathless urgency. After grabbing a head of lettuce from the fridge, she shredded a few pieces and sprinkled them on the floor for Chip.

"Cassie was at Frank's when Colt showed up. She said he looked soaked from head to toe." Eliza slid the box onto the counter before yanking open the cupboard where Penny kept the plates.

"Oh, that," Penny chuckled. "It's a long story."

"Which is why we brought *these*." Eliza flipped open the pastry box, revealing three of Maggie's jumbo-size cinnamon rolls.

Penny's stomach involuntarily grumbled, and she suddenly realized she was starving. "In that case, I'll put on a pot of tea." She quickly fetched the cast-iron kettle and filled it from the sink.

Still bursting with energy, she skipped around the kitchen.

After gathering her gold-etched Limoges tea set, she refilled the sugar bowl and creamer.

"Someone's certainly in a good mood," Eliza teased.

"You do look happy, Pen." Cassie smiled from her perch on the backless barstool. As if noticing Penny's outfit for the first time, she added, "And that's such a cute dress. But you usually wear vintage stuff. Is it new?"

"Oh, this?" Penny ran a hand along the soft fabric. "Yes, it is. Hunter gave it to me after my clothes got drenched."

"Hunter? Who's Hunter?" Eliza wiggled her eyebrows, her dark eyes glinting mischievously.

Heat creeping up her neck, Penny attempted a casual tone. "He's the owner of the ranch where we went horseback riding. He's very... nice." She fumbled over the last word, and Eliza squealed.

"You have a crush on him, don't you?"

"Of course not. Don't be silly." Turning to hide her flushed cheeks, Penny rummaged through her selection of gourmet teas.

"Yes, you do!" Eliza insisted. "It's written all over your face."

"What about Colt?" Cassie asked innocently, nibbling on the corner of a cinnamon roll.

At Cassie's question, Penny tipped over a jar of oolong, scattering the sweet-smelling leaves across the shelf. "Wh-what about him?" She tried to keep her voice steady, although her heartbeat fluttered out of control. Did Cassie know something about her brother-in-law that she didn't?

"I think she means what *happened* to Colt? You know, how did you guys get drenched?" Eliza offered, nudging Cassie with her elbow.

The gesture piqued Penny's curiosity, but she decided not to press the matter. No good could come from following that particular rabbit trail.

Settling on a rosemary and ginseng blend, Penny filled the diffuser with the fragrant leaves.

"Well..." she began, wondering how much she should share. Deciding not to gush about the perfection of the afternoon, lest they get the wrong idea, she said simply, "Things were going great until we stumbled across a rattlesnake."

"Oh no!" Cassie breathed. "How terrifying!"

"It was. My horse spooked and bolted in complete panic." Penny's pulse quickened as she recounted the story. She could still smell the dirt filling her lungs as Frost's hooves pounded the earth. In the moment, she'd been scared half to death. But when it was all over... well, she'd never felt such a rush in all her life. "Eventually,"—she continued, collecting her thoughts—"Frost stopped at the edge of the lake, bucking me into the water."

Cassie and Eliza gasped in unison, their pastries long forgotten.

"Colt dove in after me. Which is how we both got wet."

"Colt rescued you?" Eliza nearly toppled off the stool as she swooned.

"I guess you could say that...." Penny trailed off noncommittally.

"That's so romantic." Cassie pressed a hand to her heart, her green eyes soft and dreamy.

"It wasn't like that," Penny insisted swiftly.

"What happened next?" Eliza leaned halfway across the counter in her eagerness. "Did he kiss you? If this were a movie, it would totally be the part where he would kiss you."

To Penny's relief, the kettle screeched, saving her from answering Eliza's ridiculous question.

Honestly, had her friend lost her mind? Colt *kiss* her? She could say with one hundred percent certainty that it had never occurred to either of them.

Well... maybe with ninety percent certainty.

Seventy-five percent, for sure.

With a sharp shake of her head, Penny dismissed the thought.

As she poured the boiling water into the prepped teapot, she leaned forward so the steam wafted toward her face. Rosemary and ginseng were often used to promote mental clarity and prevent memory loss.

And right now, she *really* needed to remember why she'd vowed to stay single.

Otherwise, she was in danger of making a terrible mistake.

CHAPTER 11

*P*enny shivered despite the warm, eighty-degree weather.

"This isn't real... this isn't real," she whispered, gazing upward through the feathered branches of the enormous ponderosa pine.

Maybe it wasn't such a great idea to complete two of the activities back-to-back in a single weekend. At the time, she'd appreciated the strategy of knocking them off the list as quickly as possible. But now... she wanted to run home, curl up with a good book, and remain safe and sound in her snug apartment. Not tethered to a gargantuan tree at Zane's Zany Zip-Line Course—Triple Z, as locals affectionately called it.

And it certainly didn't help that mere seconds after reaching the first platform, the other couple got cold feet. The poor hysterical woman had trembled so violently, her boyfriend practically had to carry her down the ladder.

Travis, their gangly, twentysomething guide, had apologized profusely for the inconvenience, but Colt assured him they didn't mind waiting, and promised to stay clipped to the safety tether until he returned.

Talk about a huge mistake.

The longer Penny spent cowering on the platform, the more she talked herself out of jumping. Squeezing her eyes shut, she envisioned a nice, relaxing cup of peppermint tea waiting for her back home.

"You okay?" Colt nudged her gently, stirring her from her thoughts.

In reality, he'd barely tapped her. But Penny clung to the safety railing as though he'd tried to shove her to her death. She shot him a withering glare.

"I take it you're afraid of heights?"

"I'm afraid of falling from high places," she corrected, her teeth chattering. "I should have gone back when I had the chance. Do you think Travis will be upset if we climb down on our own?"

"Yes. We promised we'd stay here. Besides, you'll be fine. I've been zip-lining a hundred times. Once in Costa Rica, where the safety regulations are far less stringent than the US. And I survived."

"But you have the resilience of a cockroach. You'd probably survive the apocalypse."

"Thanks… I think," Colt chuckled, scooting closer.

The platform creaked beneath his weight, and Penny flinched. "Stop moving."

"Or what?" His eyes twinkled as he took another step toward her.

They stood shoulder to shoulder, facing the expansive tree trunk. Heat radiated from his skin as he brushed against her bare arm, and Penny sucked in a breath. "Or…"

Her comeback faltered as she gazed through the cracks in the wooden platform. The ground below blurred into shades of green and brown. They had to be at least fifty feet in the air, possibly more. And that distance would only increase as they made their way to each platform until they reached the highest and longest run at the end. The mere thought made her queasy. "I can't do this," she whimpered, her throat dry.

"Yes, you can." Colt wrapped an arm around her shoulders, offering a reassuring squeeze.

Against her better judgment, Penny huddled against his strong, muscular frame, appreciating the sense of security his presence provided.

"I'll give you a piece of advice," he offered, keeping his arm draped around her.

"If you say *don't look down*, you're going to get an elbow in your rib."

Colt laughed, and Penny found the rich, rumbling sound soothing somehow.

"I was going to say, pretend you're in a tree house, like when we were kids."

"I never played in tree houses as a kid," she confessed. "Thousands of children are treated for tree-house-related injuries each year, and my dad didn't think they were safe."

"Oh, man. I'm sorry to hear that. Luke and I used to love camping out in the tree house. Dad would usually come up for a few hours and tell us ghost stories. We never had the heart to tell him they weren't that scary." Colt's features softened at the admission. "What about you? Was your dad a fan of ghost stories?"

"Yes, but his weren't all that scary, either. Although, he did tell me one I'll never forget."

Penny closed her eyes, trying to recall every detail of that night. The steady hum of crickets harmonizing with the wind as it rustled through the dogwood branches. The scent of buttered popcorn seasoned with sumac that lingered on her fingertips. The gentle sway of the hammock as they reclined head to toe, staring up at the stars. "When I was around seven, my dad told me about a quirky inventor named Alfred Merryweather. He always wore a velvet cape and aviator goggles." She smiled at the memory, recalling the mental picture she'd built of Merryweather in her mind. "One day, he jumped from the tallest tree in

Poppy Creek on a glider made from wire coat hangers and a cotton bedsheet."

"That couldn't have ended well."

"Actually, it worked so well, he never came back down. And, according to my dad, every time a cloud floats across the sky and blocks out the sun, it's Merryweather flying by to say hello."

Colt grimaced. "Creepy."

"You think so?" Penny asked wistfully. "I always thought it was kind of beautiful."

He appeared to mull this over for a moment, his warm palm still resting on her upper arm. The sensation sent pleasant tingles dancing across her skin. "What else do you remember about your dad?"

Surprised by the question, she glanced up, meeting his gaze. His intense turquoise eyes held an undeniable tenderness, betraying his true intentions.

Her lips twitched as she hid a smile. He was actually trying to distract her from her fear of heights. A remarkably sensitive and caring gesture, especially for Colt.

"Well…" She dropped her gaze to the tips of her Converse sneakers, unnerved by the flutter in her stomach. "Dad had this unusual habit of arranging elaborate treasure hunts. He'd hide different objects around the apartment and leave me clues to find them."

"That sounds fun."

"It was." Unexpected tears pricked her eyes at the remembrance, and she quickly cleared her throat. "What about you? What's one of your favorite memories with your dad?"

"Our dad wasn't nearly as creative as yours," Colt admitted. "But he would spend hours with me in the backyard, letting me throw the football over and over again. Looking back, he must've been so bored. But he'd let me throw until my arm got tired or Mom called us in for dinner."

At Colt's soft, faraway expression, Penny's breathing slowed.

She'd never seen his sentimental side before, and it drew her to him in a way she found extremely unnerving.

"That explains why you were so good in high school," she said without thinking.

"Wait." A slow smile spread across Colt's face, revealing his dimple. "Penny Heart… did you just pay me a compliment?"

Heat swept across her cheeks, and she bit her bottom lip, embarrassed by her blunder. "Don't let it go to your head."

"Too late." His dimple deepened as he held her gaze, and suddenly, being wrapped in his arms felt far more dangerous than sailing through the trees attached to a flimsy wire.

She raised her arm to tuck a flyaway strand of hair into the confines of her safety helmet, breaking his grasp. "I just meant you weren't half bad," she said hastily. "Did you ever consider playing professionally?"

"Not really," he confessed, returning his arm to his side. "I didn't miss it as much as I thought I would when I dropped out of college."

"You found something you enjoyed more?"

"About a million other things, to be honest."

"Like jumping out of airplanes and riding a metal death trap across the county?" She'd meant for her tone to be teasing and lighthearted, but it came off as harsh and judgmental, instead.

"Is there something wrong with that?" Colt stiffened.

"No, I just meant—"

"It's okay." He attempted a smile, but it didn't quite reach his eyes. "Trust me, I get it. You're not the only one who thinks my life choices are questionable."

Regret seeped into her heart as she caught the subtle strain in his voice, although he tried to hide it.

She'd never had a problem badgering him about his reckless lifestyle before. But in the wake of the intimate moment they'd just shared, her careless quip left a sour taste in her mouth.

"Colt…." She placed her hand over his, startled by the tiny jolt of awareness that seared her skin.

Before she could say another word, Travis popped through the opening in the platform, his affable, gap-toothed grin cutting through the thick cloud of tension. "Sorry about the wait, folks. But I hope you're ready for a thrill."

An uncomfortable silence followed, and before she realized what was happening, Penny's hand shot into the air.

"I am!"

"Alrighty, then. I like the enthusiasm." Travis beamed. "Come on over."

Her legs quivering, Penny unclipped the carabiner connecting her to the tether and shuffled toward the edge of the platform. As she waited for Travis to secure her harness to the overhead cable, apprehension wrapped around her chest, making it difficult to breathe.

But remaining on the platform next to Colt proved to be even more suffocating.

She needed to get away from him in order to clear her head. Their brief, unexpected connection left her dizzier than the fifty-foot drop. Life would be so much simpler if Colt remained the irritating nuisance who called her Pepper and stuck Juicy Fruit gum in her hair.

Grown-up Colt, on the other hand, with his intriguing charm and surprising moments of sweetness, was turning out to be far too complicated for her to handle.

And if the only means of escape required sailing down a treacherous zip line…

Well, desperate times called for desperate measures.

☆

*E*ither the wind whistled especially loud inside his motorcycle helmet or Penny's petrified scream still echoed in his eardrums.

By the time they'd finished all the runs, every ounce of color had drained from her face. The entire drive home, she'd stared straight ahead, gripping the steering wheel until her knuckles blanched, not saying a word.

And when they'd parked in front of her shop, she couldn't get away from him fast enough.

Colt yanked off his helmet, struggling to muster the necessary enthusiasm for the lavish Armenian feast with Frank. He'd been looking forward to it for days, certain Frank would appreciate eating the meal as much as he'd enjoyed preparing it.

But something about the afternoon gnawed at the back of his mind. The fact was, Penny's words stung, no matter how hard he tried to blow them off.

At some point during their adventures together, he'd come to care about her opinion. More than that, he flat-out cared about *her*. And just when he'd thought maybe he stood a chance, reality smacked him in the face.

Penny still saw him as the same careless, unreliable trouble-maker she knew growing up.

And he didn't know how he'd change her mind.

Shaking the depressing thought aside, Colt registered the sights and sounds around him. Why were there so many cars in Frank's driveway? Boisterous laughter carried from the backyard along with familiar voices and a peppy, Rat Pack playlist.

Colt suppressed a groan.

He was *not* in the mood to host an impromptu barbecue.

Trudging around the side of the house, he mustered up a smile as he spotted his mother, Cassie, and Beverly playing gin rummy with Frank at the picnic table while Eliza and Ben engaged in a rowdy game of fetch with Vinny.

"'Bout time you showed up! We're starving," Jack bellowed, drawing Colt's attention to the grill where he prodded hot charcoal coals with a pair of metal tongs.

Luke, Grant, and Reed corralled around him, each sipping an ice-cold bottle of sarsaparilla.

"Your mom wouldn't even let us start with the appetizers until you showed up." Reed grinned, his pearly whites contrasting with his dark olive skin.

After his week-long gardening convention, Reed Hollis looked even more tan than usual. Which said a lot, considering he spent nearly every waking hour outside in the sun at his nursery.

Ever since he started a weed-picking business at age nine, Reed knew he wanted to work with plants—a confident assurance Colt always envied. He often wondered what it would be like to have one driving passion in life. Not that it would fit into his roving lifestyle, even if he did have one.

"And who invited you freeloaders?" Colt accepted a bottle of sarsaparilla from Luke, wiping the condensation on the hem of his T-shirt.

"Word got around you were barbecuing tonight, and I thought I'd check out the competition." Jack jabbed the tongs in the direction of Luke, Grant, and Reed. "They're here as impartial judges."

"Wait. If we're impartial, why'd you pay us twenty dollars?" Reed asked with mock seriousness.

"You're a riot, Hollis." Grinning, Jack closed the lid on the grill and turned to Colt. "All right, Davis. The coals are ready. Let's see what you're made of."

"Don't you mean, let's see what your *shish kebabs* are made of?" Grant corrected to a procession of groans and eye rolls.

"Apparently, the dad jokes have kicked in already," Colt pointed out with a good-natured grin. "But how'd you guys know I'd have enough to feed everyone?"

"Because Frank's refrigerator is stuffed with enough skewers to feed the entire town," Luke told him. "Plus, Mom made three different types of pasta and potato salads."

"And Eliza brought half the bakery for dessert." Grant's gaze drifted to his girlfriend, his smile widening as he caught sight of her wrestling in the grass with Vinny. The scruffy little devil had a death grip on an oversize rubber doughnut, but Eliza wasn't about to give up.

"I don't know how you stay in such good shape dating a baker," Reed pointed out, taking another swig of sarsaparilla.

"Yeah, when are you going to settle down and go soft like this guy?" Jack playfully elbowed Luke in his toned abs.

"Hey! I object," Luke protested, although his grin belied his offended tone.

Grant joined Jack in a good-natured laugh at Luke's expense before his attention traveled back to Eliza and their son. His features softened, practically glowing with affection, as he murmured, "Soon. And I can't wait."

Colt followed Grant's lovestruck gaze to where Eliza and Ben tousled with Vinny in the soft grass. The golden, early-evening light illuminated their joyful faces, and for a brief moment, a strange pang of envy pricked his heart.

A family wasn't in the cards for him.

And he'd never had a problem accepting that reality….

Until now.

CHAPTER 12

*a*s Colt gazed around the table at his friends and family enjoying the meal he'd prepared, his emotions vacillated between content and dissatisfied. He appreciated everyone's compliments as they gushed about how delicious everything tasted—even Frank, who seemed to be in an especially good mood that evening.

But in spite of the praise, Penny's conspicuous absence echoed above the laughter and lively conversation.

Clearing his throat, he attempted a cool, unconcerned tone. "So, where's Penny tonight?"

Eliza tilted her head, her eyes widening as though surprised he didn't already know. "When I called to invite her, she said she needed to work on the article tonight, while the events of the weekend were still fresh in her mind."

"Oh, that's right." As he took a slow, languid sip of water, a niggling voice in the back of his mind jeered, *She probably declined to avoid being around you.*

The accusation—real or imagined—weighed heavily on his heart, but he repressed the thought before it ruined the rest of the night.

"I still can't believe Penny is writing an adventure article for the town guidebook." Reed shook his head in incredulity. "She wouldn't even swim in Willow Lake when we were kids."

"Why not?" Cassie asked.

"Because of recreational water illnesses," Luke explained, helping himself to more pilaf. "Usually from parasites. They can cause skin, ear, and eye infections, stomach cramps, vomiting, diarrh—"

"Luke,"—Cassie interrupted quickly—"I love you. But if you finish that sentence, I won't be able to finish my dinner."

"Does that mean I get your leftovers?" he teased.

She shot him a playful scowl as he leaned over to kiss her cheek.

"See, that's my point," Reed continued, still baffled. "Penny and adventures don't exactly go together. Remember the time we built the ramp for our dirt bikes?" He directed his question to the guys. "Penny insisted we'd break our necks. And when we wouldn't listen, she told her dad."

"That's right!" Jack slammed his enormous palm on the table, rattling his dinner plate. "He recited a bunch of statistics about bicycle-related injuries that scared all of us except Colt."

Grant's lavender-hued eyes danced with humor as he turned toward Colt. "I have to admit, I wasn't sure you'd survive that jump."

"He almost didn't," Reed chuckled. "I've never seen anyone take such a hard spill in all my life."

"Hey!" Colt protested with a good-natured laugh. "I bet you've never seen anyone get that much air, either."

"Until you crashed, skinning both your knees so badly you wore pants the rest of summer so Mom wouldn't find out," Luke reminded him.

Maggie gaped between her two sons, her horrified gaze landing on Colt. "*That's* why you refused to wear shorts?"

Colt threw Luke a glare for spilling his secret before turning a sheepish smile on his mother. "It wasn't that bad, Mom. I promise."

"I bet he *really* wore pants so he wouldn't have to admit Penny was right about the ramp," Jack goaded.

"Possibly," Colt admitted with an impish grin.

"Especially since you promised Mr. Heart you wouldn't jump," Reed added.

At Reed's comment, Colt sensed an opening to ask a burning question. "What happened to him? Mr. Heart, I mean."

"You don't know?" Surprise flickered across Jack's face. "The story is pretty epic. He rescued a drowning tourist from Pine-drop River before getting swept away in the current."

"What?" Reed's fork paused halfway to his mouth. "I thought he died from smoke inhalation after saving an entire family from a house fire."

"No." Eliza shook her head. "He got hypothermia when a deer broke through the ice at Willow Lake and he jumped in after it."

"Actually,"—Beverly interjected softly—"it was gangrene. He got cut freeing a bear cub from a rusty trap."

Silence fell across the table as everyone exchanged bewildered glances.

"I don't understand." Cassie frowned. "All of these stories can't be true."

"Sounds like a bunch of scuttlebutt, if you ask me," Frank grumbled under his breath.

Colt scanned the group, noting the collective confusion. How was it possible no one knew how Penny's father died? It didn't make sense.

"Beverly," he said tentatively as an idea formed. "The library keeps archived copies of the *Poppy Creek Press*, right?"

"Yes…." She squinted, as though trying to follow his train of thought.

"Could you look up the obituaries from the year he died?"

"What a good idea." Her eyes brightened at the suggestion.

Cassie glanced between them. "Why don't we just ask Penny?"

"I tried to... once," Colt admitted. "She didn't want to talk about it. It's probably still a tough subject."

Cassie's face softened with sympathy. "Of course, I completely understand."

It took a while for the festive mood to recuperate as everyone returned to their meal, still perplexed over the strange turn of events.

But even as other topics of conversation came and went, Colt couldn't keep his mind from wandering to Penny.

Somewhere along the way, she'd captivated his attention, like a picturesque trail with a bend in the road, teasing his sense of curiosity and adventure.

And he wasn't entirely sure what to do about it.

***

The *click-clack* of the antique Underwood typewriter reverberated off the walls of her father's office as Penny worked on the write-up for the first two adventures.

Every few paragraphs, she took a sip of lavender tea to calm her overactive heartbeat. Reliving each activity, even by merely putting words on the page, brought back a flood of conflicting emotions.

Horseback riding had been a misleading start to the assignment, filling her with hope that had quickly been dashed by zip-lining less than twenty-four hours later.

For a brief moment, lying on the sandy bank of Chickadee Lake, she'd believed boldness resided somewhere deep inside her, untapped but waiting to burst to the surface.

For a moment, she'd finally felt free.

But today's adventure brought her crashing back to reality.

She wasn't bold. Or brave. Or adventurous.

In fact, she was quite the opposite—a boring, timid stick-in-the-mud who had no business pretending otherwise.

And until recently, she'd liked who she was—sort of.

Foolishly, she'd let Colt get inside her head, tempting her beyond her limitations.

She definitely wouldn't make that mistake again.

But somehow, she needed to find a way to survive the next activities. A task that seemed beyond impossible.

After draining the last drop of tea, Penny plucked the teacup from the matching saucer and shuffled to the kitchen for a refill. Settling herself on the barstool while she waited for the water in the kettle to boil, she gazed morosely at Chip, who basked in the glow of his heat lamp.

"What am I going to do, Chip? There are three activities left. I'll never make it."

He blinked lazily, then shuffled around so his pointed tail faced her direction.

"Okay, okay. I get it. You don't want me disturbing you in your happy place." With a huff, she placed both elbows on the kitchen counter, propping her chin in her hands. Resting her gaze on the photograph of the two young girls building a sand-castle on the beach, a smile curled her lips. Her own happy place never failed to melt the tension from her shoulders.

The first time she'd learned the concept of a *happy place*, she'd woken her dad after a particularly terrifying nightmare. She'd recited her mantra, reassuring herself the scary dream wasn't real, but she couldn't shake the dark cloud that had settled around her.

As her father put on a pot of chamomile tea, he told her to think of a happy place—somewhere the fear wouldn't be allowed to follow. And for eight-year-old Penny, the choice was easy—the ocean.

For as long as she could remember, the photograph of the sandcastle hung in their apartment. And she'd been drawn to the idyllic setting, the way the sun seemed to shine extra bright, and the water stretched on farther than her eyes could see. As an only child, she made up imaginative stories about the two girls who didn't have a care in the world. And sometimes, the stories would feel so real, she almost believed she had set foot on the sandy shore herself.

She'd never told her dad about the happy place she'd chosen. He'd told her not to, claiming it was best to keep it a secret, safely tucked away so fear could never find it. As silly as it sounded, she almost wished she *had* told him. Because then, just maybe, he could visit her there.

The kettle screeched, dragging Penny from her reverie.

As she situated herself back at the desk, the fresh cup of tea steaming by her side, she stared blankly at the typewriter.

But no words came.

Instinctively, she wrapped her hand around her upper arm, cupping the same spot where Colt had held her that afternoon. Her pulse fluttered as she recalled how comforted she'd felt tucked against him. And how for a fleeting instant, she'd forgotten all about her fear of heights, savoring the sensation of being safe in his arms.

Safe... it seemed like a foreign concept in connection with Colt. Especially since he'd roped her into a series of adventures way beyond her comfort zone. And each one only seemed to increase in risk and intensity.

In fact, merely thinking about the next activity made her palms sweat.

Popping open the secret drawer, Penny slid out her father's envelope. Holding it gently in her fingertips, she whispered, "What should I do, Dad? I'm not brave enough for this."

As the confession left her lips, a vision of Colt flashed into her mind—his eyes filled with warmth and kindness as he distracted her from the dizzying heights.

Suddenly, she realized the question for her father had nothing to do with the remaining adventures....

And everything to do with protecting her heart.

*a*s Bree helped her unpack a crate of antiques in the storage room, Penny noticed the girl's tired, swollen eyes.

"Is everything okay?" she asked gently, pushing aside the crumpled newspaper used for packing material.

"Huh?" Bree glanced up, her brow furrowed in thought.

"Do you want to talk about what's on your mind?"

Bree shook her head, her blond bob of soft finger waves grazing her shoulders.

Today's ensemble boasted 1930s-style wide-legged trousers and a cream chiffon blouse. And in Penny's opinion, it looked chic even by today's standards.

"If you change your mind, you know where to find me." While she spoke with a lighthearted tone, she hoped her warm, steady gaze communicated her sincerity.

Bree returned a faint smile in appreciation, though it didn't quite reach her seafoam-green eyes. Puffy and pink-rimmed, they held a sad glint Penny found disconcerting.

Although, on some level, she could empathize with the somber atmosphere. She'd barely slept a wink, tossing and turning until she finally slipped out of bed just before sunrise. As if she wasn't already an emotional mess after their zip-lining excursion, Colt exacerbated the issue when he asked Cassie to bring her leftovers from the barbecue. The sweet, thoughtful gesture left her even more conflicted than before.

She had no idea what to make of the man anymore. Except, he certainly wasn't the same Colt Davis she knew from her childhood. But *how* much he'd changed—and whether or not he could be trusted—was yet to be seen.

Fortunately, the mysterious crate had served as a welcome distraction from her addled musings. Around eight o'clock, she'd received a phone call from an estate sale agent wanting to unload everything that hadn't sold over the weekend. While this only happened on occasion, Penny didn't mind paying a modest fee for the items, sight unseen. Usually, she more than made her money back.

"What do you think we'll find today?" she asked, carefully unwrapping a lumpy, oddly shaped item.

"I hope some of it is vintage jewelry. Or something else that's rare and valuable." For the first time that morning, Bree's eyes brightened. "Remember when we found an old vinyl record of the Beatles? I think it was *Sgt. Pepper's Lonely Hearts Club*. A customer actually paid five hundred dollars for it. That was so cool."

"It was pretty exciting," Penny admitted, but she couldn't quite match Bree's level of enthusiasm.

The *Sgt. Pepper* reference made her think of Colt, evoking memories of the nickname he'd given her in elementary school. Why had she allowed him to get inside her head? She drew in a frustrated breath, exhaling sharply through her nose.

"Well… what is it?" Bree gave her a nudge, drawing her attention to the object in her hand.

Realizing she'd paused mid-unveiling, Penny quickly crinkled back the remaining newspaper, then instantly regretted it.

"Ew," Bree squealed, shielding her eyes from the hideous sight. "What is that thing?"

The vintage baby doll stared up at them, one eye missing, the other glazed over. Its cracked, discolored face seemed plucked straight from a horror flick.

Penny laughed at Bree's disgusted expression. "What? You don't want to take it to college with you?"

Peeking between her splayed fingers, Bree grimaced. "Not unless I want to get kicked out for being the creepiest kid on campus."

"You may have a point," Penny chuckled, rewrapping the doll in newspaper.

Bree slowly lowered her hands, her forehead scrunched, as though the burdensome thought had returned.

"You know," Penny drawled, peeling back a corner of crinkly paper. "Dolls are supposed to be great listeners...."

"Okay, okay!" Bree threw up her hands in surrender. "I'll talk. *If* you promise to hide that thing for the rest of eternity."

"Cross my heart." Hastily, Penny shoved the doll beneath a tattered lampshade before turning her full attention on Bree.

"It's just..." Bree stared at the scuffed floor, her shoulders rising and falling as she took deep, troubled breaths.

"Hold on." Removing a stack of musty linens from two Windsor dining chairs in need of mild repair, she motioned for Bree to sit down.

The girl sank onto the scratched wood with a heavy sigh. "I'm not sure I want to go to college after all."

Penny blinked. She wasn't expecting that. Bree had always sounded so excited whenever they'd discussed it before. "Why not?"

"Because..." Trailing off, she bit her bottom lip, as though afraid to say the words out loud. Finally, she murmured, "I'm scared." A shadow of shame clouded her features, and Penny reached for her hand, giving it a squeeze.

"It's okay to be scared," she said softly. "What are you afraid of?"

"Being homesick. And lonely. And... being different." Bree toyed with the flouncy ruffle on her blouse, not quite meeting her gaze.

Penny's throat constricted as the truth of Bree's fears sank in. She was afraid she wouldn't fit in. Especially with her eclectic wardrobe choices.

The poor, sweet girl. Penny's heart went out to her, but what could she say? She was the last person to espouse the ole *face your fears* mantra. If she had a choice, she'd spend her entire life avoiding them at all costs.

"You don't have to go, if you don't want to. I'm sure your parents would understand." She'd hoped the words would provide some comfort, but Bree merely looked more dejected than before.

"I guess you're right," she said weakly. "Thanks for the talk." Rising from the chair, she brushed the dust from her slacks. "Should we find out what else is in the crate?"

"Sure." Penny slowly followed, but the conversation didn't sit well.

Clearly, she'd said something wrong to elicit such an abrupt reaction, but what?

She'd offered Bree a free pass to walk away from her fears.

So why had it merely made her feel worse?

*

*R*ubbing the sleep from his eyes, Colt yawned as he followed Frank to the barn.

The cheerful sun crested the roofline of the rustic red building, casting a golden haze across the lawn, spotlighting a sprightly finch searching for breakfast. The sight would have been pleasant if he wasn't dead tired.

Considering they didn't have a single thing on the agenda for the day other than coffee roasting, Colt wasn't sure why it couldn't wait until later in the afternoon, rather than six o'clock on Monday morning.

He almost regretted staying up late to play poker with the guys. But he couldn't refuse such high stakes. Instead of chips, they'd bet with creamy, melt-in-your-mouth saltwater taffy from Sadie's Sweet Shop. Jack went home with most of it, but Colt won a few.

To be honest, his concentration wasn't really on the game. He couldn't keep his mind from wandering to thoughts of Penny. Especially after he'd received her text.

Thanks for the shish kebab. It was the best I've ever had.

Okay, so she hadn't professed her undying love, but she'd complimented his cooking. That was a start.

When he'd asked Cassie to take a plate of leftovers to Penny on her way home, he wasn't expecting to get credit for the gesture. He simply didn't want Penny to miss out on the meal because of the article. But clearly, Cassie had told her it was his idea. And he couldn't be more grateful to his sister-in-law.

The text from Penny had made his night.

Even more than the saltwater taffy.

Lost in his thoughts, Colt stumbled over a lumpy patch of grass.

"Pick up your feet, Sunshine," Frank grunted. Although, it was a more chipper-sounding grunt than usual. If a grunt could be considered chipper.

"Sorry, but I haven't had my coffee yet. And since we're on that topic... *why* aren't we having coffee first?"

"It's incentive. First, you put in the work. Then, you can have the reward. You'll appreciate it more."

"Yes, Master Yoda," Colt said with a good-natured chuckle.

"Actually, I prefer Obi-Wan." Frank paired his rebuttal with a cryptic smile, as though sharing an inside joke with himself.

Colt blinked at the unprecedented display of humor. The day was already proving to be full of surprises. And the main event hadn't even started yet.

As he slid open the barn door, Colt froze, his jaw dropping halfway to his chest. He'd expected a rinky-dink operation, not the sleek setup before him.

While the roasting machine itself appeared held together with duct tape and wishful thinking, the rest of the barn resembled a top-notch roastery—far more advanced than what he'd stumbled upon in high school.

A neat row of storage barrels flanked the back wall, each filled with green coffee beans and labeled with the country of origin—Colombia, Guatemala, Costa Rica, and Kenya, to name a few.

"I gotta say, this is pretty cool." He took in the long farm table lined with glistening, five-gallon mason jars, recalling the chapter in the book where Frank explained their role in the roasting process—mainly to sweat out the unwanted moisture from the freshly roasted beans, which both enhanced the flavor and prevented mold from forming.

As he took in the breadth of everything laid out before him, Colt's heart raced in anticipation.

"We'll see how 'cool' you think it is when the temperature in here hits the nineties." Frank shoved a bucket and large metal scoop into his hands. "Fill this with four scoops of Sumatra, four Kenya, and two Costa Rica."

"What blend are we roasting?" Colt asked, making his way to the barrel labeled Sumatra.

"Cassie's." Frank's tone carried a twinge of pride. "She came up with it one of the first times we roasted together."

"Does that mean I'll get to pick my own blend, too?" Flashing an optimistic grin over his shoulder, Colt moved to the barrel of Kenyan beans.

Frank snorted. "We'll see. You need to learn the basics first."

"Do you have all your blends written down somewhere?" As soon as the question left his lips, Colt straightened, drawing a blank on the last bean in the combination.

At his vacant expression, Frank huffed, "Two scoops of Costa Rica."

"That's right." Colt snapped his fingers before carrying the heavy bucket to the last barrel. The green beans had to weigh at least thirty pounds.

As he filled the remainder of the bucket, Frank settled himself in a wicker chair by the roasting machine. "To answer your question, Cassie is helping me write down all the blends."

"Is that what your new book is about?"

"Partly. But the main goal is to teach other roasters how to create their own blends. How to recognize the different flavor profiles of each bean and what pairs well together."

"Huh." Colt cocked his head. "Kind of like knowing which ingredients to combine when cooking."

"Yes." A brief flicker of approval darted across Frank's face before he replaced it with a stoic frown. "Now, we siphon the beans into the machine."

As Frank verbally walked him through each stage of the roasting process, Colt marveled at the numerous similarities to his culinary education. Pairing the various beans, roasting temperature and duration—each step was designed to enhance the flavor and mouthfeel; a delicate dance between chemistry and art. And Colt found himself captivated by every minute detail.

He didn't care that he'd started to sweat, both from the heat and exertion. Or that Frank hadn't stopped barking orders since he'd loaded the beans into the machine.

They'd finished Cassie's blend, plus two espresso roasts for the café, and Colt wasn't even close to losing interest.

"What about a blonde roast?" he asked, eager to learn more. "Can we do one of those next?"

Frank's expression darkened.

"I take it you're not a fan."

"And why would I be a fan of sour coffee?"

"Doesn't it have more caffeine?"

"You want caffeine? Drink green tea. You want good coffee, then roast it properly,"—Frank grumbled, adding—"Anything worth doing, should be done right. You're either all in or you're out. We'll do Cassie's blend again and see how much you remember."

As Colt strode to the barrel of Sumatra, Frank's words tumbled in his mind.

You're either all in or you're out.

Frank was right.

And not just about the coffee.

CHAPTER 14

*a*s Penny stood on the rocky bank of Pinedrop River, a chill ran through her despite the late afternoon sun. If only she could take her own advice and run far, far away from her present fear, back to the safety of the familiar.

But she didn't have that luxury, unless she wanted to disappoint Beverly.

"Nervous?" Colt peered down at her, concern etched into his tanned forehead.

"Why do you ask? Can you hear my teeth chattering?" She tried to muster a playful laugh, but it caught in her throat.

"Kind of, yeah." He flashed his dimpled smile. But rather than impish and teasing, it radiated a warm, sympathetic quality that caused her pulse to quicken.

Her hands clenched around the smooth handle of her oar as she directed her gaze to their guide—a lean, muscular woman with long blond dreadlocks tied in an orange bandana on top of her head. No matter how many times she'd assured Penny that white water rafting was perfectly safe, Penny couldn't calm her rampant heartbeat. It pounded in her ears above the rumble of the river as it charged downstream with deadly urgency.

"Do you think Roxie knows what she's doing?" Penny watched the guide go over last-minute details with a young trainee by the water's edge.

"Without a doubt," Colt said with confidence. "She's rafted the class-five rapids of Futaleufú River in Chile twice."

"And class five… that's pretty difficult?"

"Oh, yeah. The one time I did that run, I barely made it out alive."

The laughter in his voice didn't quite match the severity of his words. He must have noticed her horrified expression, because his features instantly softened. "You'll be fine, I promise. Roxie is the best guide they've got. Plus, you have me."

Penny frowned. "No offense, but that's supposed to assuage my fears because…"

"Because I'd never let anything bad happen to you."

The serious glint in his eyes caused her breath to falter. Swallowing hard, she dropped her gaze to the tips of her rubber-soled water shoes.

As their group loaded into the flimsy-looking raft, Penny's stomach flipped. She'd feel much safer if it resembled an actual boat, with a sturdy floor and tall, protective sides. Instead, they'd be barreling down raging rapids in a glorified inner tube.

Her legs froze, unable to propel her body forward.

Colt appeared behind her and placed a reassuring hand on her lower back. "Sit on the starboard side." He tipped his head toward the right side of the raft. "I'll sit behind you."

Penny followed his direction, cringing as the pliable material shifted under her weight. What would it take to poke a hole in the bottom? A sharp rock? A wayward stick? She nervously gnawed her lower lip as she settled behind a teenage boy who seemed amped up on too much sugar and youthful naivete.

Growing up, Penny never bought into the childish belief of invincibility. Her father raised her to assess the risk in everything, prioritizing safety first and foremost. When other parents were teaching their children not to run with scissors, her dad extolled the virtues of a brisk walk, and never while holding a pointed object of any kind. Unless you *wanted* to poke an eye out.

Penny flinched as the remainder of their party got situated, bobbing the raft up and down as the soles of their shoes squeaked against the thick rubber. Counting herself and Colt, the guide and trainee, a middle-aged father and his teenage son, and a giddy couple on their honeymoon, their group totaled eight.

Another raft of eight set out a few minutes ahead of them and a third would follow shortly after. Then, assuming they all survived, they'd enjoy a simple barbecue and s'mores in the evening.

But presently, even the thought of food made Penny queasy.

After Roxie doled out a few more safety reminders—using rafting lingo that sounded like a foreign language—Penny sucked in a breath as they set off on their foolhardy adventure.

For the first few minutes, the current carried them along at a peaceful pace, and she found the rhythmic refrain of the oars splashing into the water rather soothing.

But as they rounded a bend in the river, her pulse spiked, matching the uptick in the current's intensity. The raft lurched over rough waves, dousing her arms and legs with a chilly spray.

Fear crawled up her spine, and she jolted as Colt laid a comforting hand on her shoulder. "Are you okay? If you're too scared to row, set the oar in the bottom of the boat, and I'll pick up the slack."

Nodding gratefully, she tucked the oar by her feet and gripped the rope so amusingly dubbed the *chicken line*.

As they thrashed in the water, pummeled on all sides by unrelenting waves, everyone but Penny seemed to be having the time of their lives. Hoots, hollers, and peals of laughter collided in a cacophony of boisterous excitement as they hurdled toward their inevitable demise.

How on earth could they be enjoying this? Didn't they realize it was the preamble to their eventual doom? Surely, she couldn't be the only rational person on board. Glancing over her shoulder, she gaped at the look of pure exhilaration plastered across Colt's handsome features.

"Woo-hoo!" he shouted with an inexplicable grin as a frigid spray drenched his face. He wiped the water from his eyes with his sinewy forearm, before deftly dipping the oar back into the torrent. The muscles in his biceps flexed against the strain, but Colt appeared to be loving every single second, as though he were built for this precise moment.

Her neck craned, she watched, completely mesmerized, as his body rocked back and forth, in tune with the violent throws of the river. How did he look so at peace in the midst of the chaos?

"Try it!" he shouted over the thunderous roar.

Penny blinked, startled from her trance. "Try what?"

"Hoot, holler, howl… let loose."

"No, thanks." She shook her head, flinging water droplets from her loose strands of hair.

"C'mon," he cajoled. "Try it one time. It'll help. I promise."

She squinted at him dubiously. But, then again… what could it hurt? She was already terrified out of her mind. It couldn't make things any worse.

Swiveling back around, she inhaled deeply, filling her lungs with a rush of crisp air. Could she actually do this? Letting loose wasn't exactly in her repertoire.

Before she could change her mind, she tilted her head back and bellowed, "Woo-hoo!" with every ounce of strength she possessed.

Tension escaped with her words, replaced by a surge of endorphins.

"Thatta girl!" Colt whooped in approval.

Laughing, she tried again, projecting from deep within herself. And to her delight, everyone else in the raft joined in, as if cheering her on.

Bolstered by their support and her newfound bravery, she reached for the oar, determined to pull her own weight. But the second she let go of the chicken line, the raft plunged over a steep drop. Roxie shouted for everyone to hold on, but Penny wasn't quick enough. They smacked into the pool below, the force of impact launching Penny from her seat.

Before she could process what happened, icy water filled her nose and mouth, shocking her senseless. Buoyed by her life vest, she broke through the surface and heaved in a desperate gasp for air along with another mouthful of water.

White-tipped waves smacked her face, their harsh sting bringing tears to her eyes.

This is how she would die. And she'd never even been in love.

Overcome with emotion, she wanted to cry, but the glacial temperatures and crippling fear left her too numb to do anything but try not to drown. And so far, she wasn't doing a great job.

"Lawn chair!"

Completely disoriented, she thought she heard Colt shouting something, but it didn't make any sense.

"Lawn chair!" The strange command came again, more urgent this time. But what did it mean? Was it possible she'd passed out and was experiencing a delirious dream? Wasn't her life supposed to flash before her eyes? Instead, she got an incoherent hallucination. *Just her luck.*

"Lean back and bend your knees!" the figment of her imagination shouted.

Suddenly, a hazy memory of Roxie's safety briefing sprang to her mind and on impulse, she quickly obeyed.

The new position gave her instant relief from the bitter surge trying to force her under.

"Hang on. I'm going to get you out of here." Like a vision, Colt appeared by her side, linking his arm with hers.

"There's a fallen log protruding from the bank up ahead," he hollered over the deafening swell. "I'm going to steer us toward it, but I need you to work with me, okay?"

The river continued to drag them downstream at an alarming rate, and Penny stared into his unflinching gaze, unable to speak. Was this really happening? What was he doing here?

"We're going to be okay. But I need you to trust me. Can you do that?"

Without hesitation, she nodded.

"Good. Don't fight the current. It'll wear you out. We'll gradually work our way toward the edge. Just stay with me."

After what felt like hours of struggle, but probably only lasted a few minutes, Colt latched on to a branch, summoning all his strength to pull them toward the log and out of the swift current.

"Hang on. The raft will be here any second."

As Penny clung to the massive tree trunk, Colt's muscular arm braced around her shivering body, the reality of the situation washed over her.

Colt Davis had just saved her life.

CHAPTER 15

*T*he fire crackled, sending amber sparks flitting into the obsidian sky. An endless swath of glittering stars canopied Pinedrop Rafting's base camp, while an army of silhouetted pines stood guard around the perimeter. Although she could still hear the rumble of the river through the trees, she felt safe here—protected. But her sense of security had less to do with her sheltered location and everything to do with the man standing just beyond the campfire, surrounded by fellow rafters eager to recount the details of his heroic rescue.

She still couldn't believe he'd jumped into the dangerous current, risking his life to save hers. And each time he looked past the crowd of gushing fans to catch her eye, her stomach fluttered.

"You are *so* lucky." A young twentysomething woman wearing a hot-pink tank top emblazoned with the words *Team Bride* plopped onto the log beside her and snatched the bag of marshmallows. "Your boyfriend is a hero *and* superhot."

"We were on the raft behind you guys." A petite brunette with a matching tank top squeezed onto the log between them, nearly stabbing Penny with her s'more skewer. "I wish we'd been close enough to see the whole thing go down. I heard he didn't even hesitate before diving into the river after you."

Tugging the wool blanket tighter around her shoulders, Penny shuffled over a few inches to give them room. She thought about correcting their assumption that she and Colt were a couple. But rather than have the entire bachelorette party converge on him like a swarm of flirtatious bees, she merely smiled and focused on her slowly browning marshmallow.

"I wonder if Ansel would do the same thing for me." The bride —as denoted by her white tank top—puckered her lips in a contemplative pout.

"Of course he would!" her posse rushed to assure her. Although, she didn't look entirely convinced.

A twig snapped, drawing their attention to the other side of the campfire.

"He's coming over here," the brunette squealed under her breath.

"Come on, ladies. Let's give the lovebirds some privacy." With an authoritative sweep of her hand, the bride gathered her dutiful followers to the second firepit, tossing Penny a wink over her shoulder as she waggled her ring finger suggestively.

Flustered, Penny diverted her gaze into the bright flames, hoping the heat would camouflage her telltale blush as Colt approached.

"Still working on the same marshmallow?" he asked with a playful smile.

"I like to take my time." She glanced up, meeting his gaze, and instantly regretted the decision. His mesmerizing blue eyes radiated a tender warmth that traveled all the way to the tips of her toes.

"You're a fan of the slow-and-steady approach, huh?" He settled on the log next to her, so close their thighs touched. Her heart raced as he reached across her for a skewer and marshmallow. His heady scent mixed with the smoky aroma of burning cedar and smoldering pine needles, overwhelming her senses to the point of distraction.

She swallowed past the sudden dryness in her throat. "Let me guess, you shove your marshmallow straight into the nearest flame?"

"I'm not afraid to go all in, if that's what you mean. But I'm willing to try it your way." He maneuvered his roasting stick toward the same patch of coals, angling his marshmallow a few millimeters from hers.

The fire seemed to burn hotter, somehow. And despite her still damp clothes and the cool night air, she almost didn't need the wool blanket anymore.

"Is there enough to share?" To her surprise, Colt gestured to the soft plaid fabric wrapped around her shoulders. Had he read her mind?

"My board shorts are fine, but this T-shirt refuses to dry." He pulled at the ribbed cotton clinging to his broad chest, inviting her gaze to his well-defined muscles.

She gulped. "Um, sure." Holding out the corner, her breath faltered as he scooted closer, his knee grazing hers.

What was happening to her? Her insides felt gooier than the center of her marshmallow.

Was she falling for this man?

Or was it possible that she already had?

*

What was he doing?

Asking Penny to share the blanket as an excuse to get closer was a rookie move. And he didn't play games. He spoke his mind, especially when it came to women.

But with Penny, things were different. His usual confidence and bravado wavered. He actually felt nervous. At least, he assumed nerves explained the tight clench in his stomach and the erratic racing of his heartbeat.

He needed to be direct. *Just tell her how you feel.*

As he gave himself a pep talk, he stole a glance in her direction. *Big mistake.* The sight of her profile—a stunning silhouette highlighted by the arresting glow of the fire—caused his breath to lodge somewhere between his lungs and his throat, constricting his chest uncomfortably.

Yeesh. Being around this woman had turned him inside out *and* upside down. He didn't know what to do with himself.

Sitting this close to her, he could count the adorable freckles scattered across the bridge of her nose. And he found himself even more captivated by the alluring trail they forged down the delicate curve of her neck and across her slender shoulders. He resisted the urge to graze them with his rough palm.

Forcing his attention on the roasting marshmallows, he racked his brain for safe topics of conversation. Anything to keep his mind off kissing her. Penny was a slow-and-steady kind of girl. Which meant he needed to be patient and take his time—a foreign concept outside the culinary realm. He could braise lamb shanks all day. But patiently and purposefully pursue a woman? That would be a first.

But without question, Penny was worth the wait. The moment she'd fallen overboard, he knew his life would never be the same. His entire world had stopped in that split second.

For the first time, he knew what it meant to care about a woman more than himself. And he would do anything to protect her. Even if it meant protecting her from himself.

"I'm sorry about what happened today," he said quietly, rotating the marshmallow over the coals.

"It wasn't your fault."

"Maybe not, technically. But river rafting was my idea. I swear, if I thought it was unsafe, I—"

"It's okay." To his surprise, she smiled softly, a teasing glint in her coppery eyes. "I think your actions today proved you aren't actually *trying* to kill me."

His heart sputtered, once again amazed by her ability to find the humor in a difficult situation. "Glad to hear it. But I completely understand if you don't want to go through with the rest of the activities on the list."

Colt held his breath as she stared into the fire, the pop and crackle of the embers filling the silence.

Finally, she met his gaze. "I'd like to keep going, if that's okay with you."

He blinked, taken aback by her response. Truthfully, he'd expected her to quit. And after today, he wouldn't blame her. "Are you sure?"

She nodded, fixing her eyes back on her marshmallow. The lightly browned crust looked perfectly golden, but she kept it over the coals, appearing lost in her thoughts. "You know how they say your life flashes before your eyes when you have a near-death experience?"

"Yeah." His marshmallow started to bubble and slide off the end of his stick, but he didn't dare disrupt her next words.

"Well... it's partly true. Unless you don't have many experiences to reflect on." She turned toward him, a slight smile curling her lips. "Don't get me wrong. I'm not saying I'll become a dare-devil like you. But I *would* like a few more adventures under my belt for the next end-of-life montage."

She held his gaze, her features an alluring array of newfound fortitude and fragile vulnerability.

His fingers ached to smooth back the wayward strands of auburn hair, crimped and wild after the confines of her French braid. Every single detail of her physical appearance seemed fashioned from his unspoken ideal. And yet, it wasn't her outward beauty that made him breathless.

Her quiet strength had captivated him, heart and soul.

And taught him that being fearless is far less noble than doing the things that make you afraid.

He swallowed past the roughness in his throat. "Then let's make sure that montage is Oscar-worthy."

His gaze instinctively fell to her mouth, and every nerve in his body tingled as she slowly parted her lips, giving him a subtle green light.

With bated breath, he inched forward, his heartbeat hammering in his ears.

Penny's eyelids fluttered closed.

As he lowered his head, a sudden hiss and sizzle dragged their attention to the fire.

Both their marshmallows had plopped onto the coals and burst into flames.

Much like their perfect moment.

CHAPTER 16

*F*or most of the night, Penny lay awake, staring up at the canopy of colorful tapestries draped above her bed. The soothing hum of ocean waves caressing the coastline emanated from her sound machine, but it did little to calm her restlessness.

Every time she drifted off to sleep, she had the same terrifying nightmare.

The river's tumultuous current swept her toward a thundering waterfall, fallen tree branches shattering against sharp rocks jutting from the deep, murky pool below.

Colt appeared by her side and grasped her hand. But rather than lead her to safety, he whooped in excitement, assuring her the ride over the falls would be the biggest thrill of her life.

As the water swelled, pushing her toward the edge, she glanced at Colt for reassurance. But he'd disappeared, leaving her utterly alone.

She woke in the fetal position, the cotton sheets tangled around her legs.

Even after the third rendition, the dream ended the same

exact way—Penny sailing over the edge; her petrified scream her only companion.

After wiping beads of sweat from her forehead, she rolled over to check the time on her phone—4:00 a.m.

With a frustrated sigh, she clicked off her sound machine and wrestled free from the covers.

There were only two more activities left. Despite her brave proclamation that she needed more adventures under her belt, she must be getting cold feet. That had to explain the dream, didn't it?

Slipping out of bed, she padded barefoot into the kitchen to put on the teakettle—sans the steam whistle since she didn't want the loud screech so early in the morning.

While she waited for the water to boil, she slumped over the counter, gazing into her favorite photograph.

Normally, she focused on the peaceful imagery of the azure sea hugging the pristine shoreline. But today, her focus drifted to the sandcastle, dwelling on the conflicting symbolism.

On one hand, a castle could be a fortress or a sanctuary—an indomitable means of protection. And yet... it could also be a prison, where captives were either locked in a tower or thrown into a bleak dungeon.

Penny squinted at the photograph, visually tracing the outline of the high walls and cylindrical turrets. What was *her* castle? A sanctuary or a prison cell?

Her gaze drifted to the surrounding moat, at least six inches wide and a foot deep. But was it supposed to keep someone in or out?

The rumble of boiling water at the bottom of the kettle pulled Penny from her philosophical musings.

As she waited for her coconut chai tea to steep, images of the white-capped waves and heart-stopping plunge invaded her mind. But what haunted her the most wasn't what she could see. But rather, what she *couldn't* see.

Colt had deserted her on the crest of the waterfall.

Shivering from a nonexistent chill, she asked aloud, "What do you think it means?" more to herself than anyone in particular.

Chip's eyelids flitted open briefly before he burrowed deeper into his enclosure.

"Sorry." Penny pulled an apologetic face for waking him.

Quietly gathering her teacup, she crept into her father's office and gently latched the door behind her. Settling at his desk, she popped open the secret compartment. The smooth white envelope felt pleasantly cool to the touch, and she pressed it to her collarbone, closing her eyes.

"I don't know what to do, Dad. Do you think I can trust him?"

She received no response, save for the haunting call of a lone owl in the distance.

But even without hearing her dad's voice, she suspected his answer.

Giving someone your heart required the biggest risk of all.

And it hadn't turned out well for her father.

Penny was five years old the first time she asked about her mother. She had no memories of ever having one, but according to the other kids in school, every child did, at one time or another.

That's when she learned her mother wasn't a boring ole human mom like all the other kids had. But a magical being more beautiful than any woman on earth, with huge, birdlike wings and a singing voice so mesmerizing, she could use it to cast spells.

One evening, her father found her mother trapped in the forest, her large wings pinned by a fallen branch. She was so grateful he'd rescued her, she offered to take him on a flight around the world. He said they fell in love among the stars.

A few months later, they married in the chapel on top of the hill, and she seemed happy in Poppy Creek, for a time. Especially after having Penny. But eventually, she grew restless. *That's the problem with having wings*, her father had said. *You need somewhere to fly.*

Of course, as she grew older, she knew the fanciful story couldn't be true. And she also learned her father's brave face was only a mask disguising the truth, much like his fairy tale.

But she only saw him without his mask once, when she was nine. In the middle of the night, she woke to a stirring sound coming from the balcony. Tiptoeing to the French doors, she eased one open and peered through the crack. Her father clutched an emerald and ruby brooch, the gems glittering in the moonlight. As he gazed at the stars, silent tears trailed down his cheeks. And even though she'd outgrown the childish tale about the woman with feathered wings, for the briefest of moments, she wondered if he was out on the balcony hoping to catch one last glimpse.

And that's when she realized all the love in the world couldn't make someone stay.

Especially if they wanted to fly.

*A*fter yesterday's harrowing experience and several hours of roasting coffee, Colt expected to feel drained—mentally and physically. But when it came to his newfound passion, he seemed to have an endless reserve of energy. Each stage of the process enthralled him, and he wanted to learn as much as possible. Ultimately, he hoped to earn Frank's trust so he could develop his own blend. He already had a few ideas, but whenever he broached the subject, Frank would insist he wasn't ready.

After their last roast of the day, Colt's entire body ached—a memento of a hard day's work. In the downtime while the beans circulated in the chamber of hot air, Frank had him refill the barrels. Each sack of green beans had to weigh over a hundred pounds. And rather than scoop the beans into the barrel by hand —which would have taken forever—Colt employed a shortcut, lifting each sack and dumping the contents. While much quicker, his lower back paid the price.

At the very least, all the manual labor served as a distraction. He struggled to keep his mind off Penny, wondering how she was doing after the previous day's adventure. Not to mention their almost-kiss. Every time he closed his eyes, he envisioned the outline of her perfect lips, and couldn't help wondering if they tasted as incredible as he imagined.

Shaking the spine-tingling thought from his mind, Colt grabbed a broom to sweep the spilled coffee beans into a neat pile. His muscles groaned even under the menial task.

Although Frank operated on a much smaller scale before Cassie opened The Calendar Café, Colt still marveled at the man's stamina, especially for his age. And with the increase in demand ever since they created an online store, he wasn't sure how Frank would keep up long-term, even with Cassie's help.

He cast a concerned glance in Frank's direction. He'd remained in the rocking chair, a few feet from the action, most of the afternoon, supervising Colt's roasting education. And yet, his weathered features displayed signs of fatigue and strain. Fortunately, he'd get a break tomorrow while Colt completed the fourth adventure with Penny.

As the thought sprang to mind, he couldn't help a reflexive smile.

"Who is she?"

Startled by Frank's unexpected question, Colt blinked. "What?"

"The smile on your face… who's the girl?"

"It's that obvious, huh?"

"I'm old, but I'm not blind. I know a man in love when I see one."

The handle slipped from Colt's grasp, clattering to the

ground. Rattled, he scrambled to recover the broom, disturbing his neat mound of coffee beans in the process.

Frank chuckled. "No need to get your knickers in a knot. I take it you haven't said the *L* word yet?"

"No, I... we haven't... what I mean is..." Thoroughly flummoxed, Colt stood stock-still, his jaw hanging open. *In love?* He knew he cared about Penny. More than anyone. And he would do anything for her. But love? He wasn't even sure he knew what that meant. At least, not completely.

The lyrics from the old nursery rhyme "The Kissing Song" popped into his head, and he started to sweat. *First comes love, then comes marriage...*

"Relax, son." Frank's features softened. "Your secret is safe with me. But can I give you a piece of advice from one fool to another?"

"Sure," Colt croaked, tugging on his shirt collar. The temperature inside the barn must've increased by a hundred degrees.

"You get one shot at this life. And each day that passes, you only get older. Until you're one dance away from it being your last." Frank's voice took on a husky quality, as though his throat had constricted around his words. "If you've found your partner, don't waste a single second hemming and hawing. You spin her around that dance floor never once forgetting that you're the luckiest man alive."

As Frank spoke, Colt recalled glimpses of Frank and Beverly waltzing across the dance floor at Luke and Cassie's wedding, moments before his heart attack. And he couldn't help wondering why Frank didn't take his own advice.

He clearly loved Beverly, yet chose to live alone. And until recently, had cut himself off from everyone in town. Growing up, he'd always pitied Frank Barrie's reclusive lifestyle. And yet, was his life all that different?

Sure, he traveled the world, experiencing adventures most people couldn't even fathom.

But what would it be like to share them with someone else? Especially someone he loved....

a s he fidgeted with the setting on his headlamp, Colt stole a surreptitious glance in Penny's direction.

A lot rode on today's adventure, and he wanted to make sure she felt safe and comfortable. And maybe even enjoyed herself.

"How are you feeling?" He studied her expression closely.

"Okay, I think. We're not likely to drown in a cave, right?" Her gaze darted to the ominous entrance, a thin worry line etched across her forehead.

"The chances are slim." He flashed a reassuring smile as he handed her a headlamp.

"What's this for?" she asked, tugging on the elastic strap.

"I like to bring my own light. The ones provided by the tour guides are dim and unreliable. I keep two headlamps in my ready bag at all times in case one of the batteries goes out."

"What's a 'ready bag'?"

"It's a backpack I keep fully stocked with an assortment of supplies for when an unexpected adventure presents itself."

"Why am I not surprised you'd have something like that?" Penny chuckled softly.

At the pleasant lilt of her laugh, warmth radiated throughout his body. He could get used to hearing that sound. "Just loop it over your head and press the top button to turn the light on and off," he explained with a quick demonstration.

After securing the lamp to her safety helmet, she practiced the movement, inadvertently blinding him.

"Hey! Careful with that thing." With a good-natured grimace, he shielded his eyes from the harsh beam of light.

"Oops." Penny clicked it off, then waited for him to lower his guard before switching it back on again, giggling as he flinched in surprise. "This is going to be fun." She tossed him a mischievous grin before turning toward the tour guide who was busy gathering the rest of their group.

Colt shook his head in bemusement, happy to see her in such good spirits.

"For those of you entering through the main entrance, make your way over to Brian." The lithe older gentleman gestured toward a younger, heavyset guide who gave them an enthusiastic wave. "The rest of you, follow me. We'll meet up in the last cavern, which we affectionately call the Concert Hall."

Penny moved toward Brian's group, but Colt placed a hand on her elbow. "Not that way."

She stared up at him, wide-eyed. "We're not going through the main entrance?"

"Nope." His pulse quickened as he led her behind the handful of would-be spelunkers following Martin—their spry, sinewy guide clad in a full-body rappelling harness.

Either this would go very well or horribly wrong. There didn't seem to be much room in the middle. Colt said a silent prayer against every worst-case scenario.

Their small group clustered around a large hole in the ground surrounded by a sturdy safety railing, palpable excitement rippling through the air. A young girl with braided pigtails peered over the edge, disturbing the loose earth with the tip of her sneakers. The pebbles disappeared into the darkness without a sound.

Penny gasped by his side. "We're going down *there*." She said the last word as though they were climbing into the mouth of an active volcano.

"It's not as scary as it looks." He placed a comforting hand on her shoulder. "And I'll be with you the whole time."

Penny glanced up, meeting his gaze. Her coppery eyes searched his a moment, as if gauging his sincerity. Finally, she managed a small smile. "Okay."

"Who's first?" Martin grabbed a harness from the nearby rack.

The girl—who couldn't have been more than twelve or thirteen—jumped up and down, flapping her arm above her head as she squealed with youthful enthusiasm.

Penny studied the scene with evident interest as Martin helped the eager child and her father get set up with the appropriate rigging based on their individual weight and size.

"Penny for your thoughts?" Colt asked playfully.

She made a face at his cheesy pun before her features softened. "I was just thinking, my dad never would have brought me to something like this."

"Do you wish he had?"

"I'm honestly not sure," she admitted. "Until recently, I'd never thought about it." Tilting her head to the side, she asked, "What about you? Was your dad into this kind of stuff?"

Colt's heartbeat thundered against his rib cage as if pushing him to tell her his long-kept secret. His father's dying words rested on the tip of his tongue, waiting to be shared, until a gleeful shriek severed their intimate connection.

As the girl and her father vanished into the cave below, Penny seized his hand, squeezing with all her might.

"Don't worry. I've got you." He tightened his grip to punctuate his point.

"Who's next?" Martin asked.

Colt glanced down at Penny. "Ready?"

Keeping her claim on his hand, she gave a tentative nod.

As they took a step forward together, Colt couldn't help wondering if their next step would define their entire future.

And if he was prepared for where it might take him.

As Martin helped Penny into her harness and set up her rigging, Colt kept a keen eye on her facial expressions and body language. Her slender shoulders seemed particularly tight and every few seconds, she nibbled her bottom lip.

Her gaze briefly flitted to his as she slipped on their last item of safety gear—thick gloves designed to protect their hands from rope burn.

"Remember, you'll step backward into the hole," Martin reminded them. "And what's the number one rule?"

"Never let go of the rope." Colt recited the words with an authoritative tone earned by years of experience.

"Not your first time, I take it?" Martin asked.

"I haven't explored the Dark Star in Uzbekistan yet, but I've rappelled nearly every pit in Ellison's Cave and spent two weeks off-grid in Nepal with a local guide."

Duly impressed, Martin tipped his head at Penny. "You're in good hands, miss." He stepped back to man their rigging, giving Colt the go-ahead to descend.

"Okay, this is it." Colt locked eyes with Penny. "I'll be right beside you the entire time."

Her features ashen, she reached for his hand again. "Please, don't let go."

He glanced at their entwined fingers. Holding hands while rappelling into a cavern wasn't exactly common procedure. But she peered at him with such intense earnestness, he couldn't bring himself to decline her request. "I won't," he promised. "Just keep your other hand on the rope the whole way down."

"Okay," she said dutifully, nearly crushing his knuckles with her tight grip.

For a split second, Colt regretted the heavy gloves, longing to feel her soft skin against his and the warmth of her palm. Clearing his head with a swift shake, he leaned back. "On my count, push off the wall."

Still gnawing her bottom lip, she nodded wordlessly in response.

As he began the countdown, the familiar swell of adrenaline filled his veins, heightening his senses. But this time, something felt different.

He cast a sideways glance at Penny and caught her watching him intently, as if ensuring he was still there. Grinning, he gave her hand one last squeeze before shouting, "Three!" He kicked off the rough stone, sending them sailing backward into the abyss.

Penny screamed. But rather than the sharp cry of terror he'd expected, her trill of exhilaration reverberated off the walls, making his heart soar.

Every adventure he'd ever experienced—from free diving with tiger sharks in the Bahamas to biking Death Road in Bolivia —paled in comparison to this moment.

And it had everything to do with the woman holding his hand.

⭐

*H*er feet firmly planted on the ground, Penny drew in a deep breath, relishing the heady scent of damp sediment. "That was incredible!"

"It sure was."

At Colt's husky tone, Penny's gaze dropped to their fingers, still woven together. Her cheeks flushed despite the cool temperature inside the expansive cavern.

He hadn't let go. Not even once, throughout their entire descent.

She lifted her eyes to meet his, and an emotionally charged look passed between them.

"Well done, folks." The guide's monotone voice betrayed her boredom—and her blindness to their heart-stopping glance.

Suddenly self-conscious, Penny released her grasp, immediately missing Colt's touch.

Smacking her chewing gum—which had to be contraband in such a transcendent place—the girl assisted them in removing their rappelling gear. "You continue through that tunnel for the next phase of your adventure." She listlessly gestured toward a narrow passageway, and Penny marveled at how anyone could lose interest in what appeared to be a magical world where anything was possible.

"Ready?" Colt clicked on his headlamp, illuminating even more of the fantastical space.

The jagged walls glistened with moisture, amplifying the ethereal atmosphere. Switching on her own light, she gazed upward, bewitched by the dazzling stalactites dripping from the ceiling like icicles melting in the late afternoon sun.

For a moment, Penny lost the ability to breathe, only reviving when Colt slipped his fingers through hers, sending jolts of electricity coursing up her arm.

"Let's go." His words hummed with excitement as he tugged her toward the sliver in the wall.

Her heart undulated. "We have to crawl through there? It hardly seems wide enough."

"If I can fit, you'll glide right through." Something in his smile steadied her pulse, and she grinned back.

"Lead the way."

CHAPTER 18

*A*s she shimmied through the tight crevice behind Colt, Penny's chest constricted, and it took all her willpower not to hyperventilate.

"We're almost there," Colt announced with confident assurance. "And once we get to the other side, it'll all be worth it."

Drawing in a shaky breath, she pushed forward.

The oppressive walls seemed to close in around her, making it increasingly difficult to breathe. She wasn't sure how much longer she could take the confined space, but keeping her headlight trained straight ahead provided a modicum of comfort. As long as she could keep the end in sight, she would be okay.

As soon as the reassuring thought crossed her mind, she felt something brush against her leg. With a terrified squeal, she jumped, whacking her headlamp against the cold, hard stone. A horrifying *crunch* preceded immediate darkness.

Great! There were probably killer spiders lurking in the tunnel and she'd just broken her only source of light.

Frantic, she stretched her fingertips into nothingness. "C-Colt?"

"I'm here." Farther down the tunnel, he craned his neck to

glance over his shoulder, illuminating her face. "Are you okay?"

"I'm not sure. I think I felt a spider or something. And I accidentally broke your headlamp."

"Come closer. We still have mine." As he tapped his bulb, it suddenly went out.

"That's not funny," she chided through clenched teeth.

"I'm so sorry, Pen." His tone was deathly serious. "My battery must've died."

"Please tell me you're joking," she whimpered in the darkness.

"I'm afraid not. But don't worry, we're almost at the end. And another group should be coming through this way soon."

On the verge of panic, Penny drew in a shallow breath, following the comforting beacon of Colt's voice.

Her legs trembled as they crept onward, the sound of shuffling sediment filling the silence.

After what felt like hours—though likely only lasted a few minutes—the air shifted, free and unfettered by the impenetrable barricade of limestone.

But Penny could only guess that they'd made it to the next cavern. Without a shred of light, she couldn't be sure of anything.

Reaching for Colt blindly, she staggered forward, stumbling on the uneven ground. She cried out before being caught up in strong, steady arms.

"Are you okay?" They stood so close his breath caressed her forehead.

Startled by the instant jolt of awareness, she couldn't speak, barely managing an imperceptible nod.

"Pen, are you all right?" As he repeated the question, his voice sounded deep and gravelly, and Penny felt the vibration all the way to the tips of her toes.

She swallowed hard. "Yes." The solitary word escaped in a throaty sigh, and she was suddenly conscious of Colt's rough fingertips traveling the length of her bare arm, causing every inch of her body to tingle.

Something about standing mere inches apart in utter blackness made Penny more aware of his scent—the way it enticed her like an invigorating gust of ocean wind. And how his rich timbre resembled the soothing rumble of powerful waves against the shore.

She could no longer deny the pull he had over her, a rip current that could so easily drag her out to sea. Her heart fluttered as his left hand slid around her waist, finding its home against the small of her back.

"This isn't real," she whispered, recalling the prevailing wisdom to survive a rip current—don't fight it.

"Are you sure?" Colt murmured. His skillful fingertips worked their way up her arm to explore the nape of her neck, as though, even in darkness, their bodies were completely in tune.

Following the sound of his voice, Penny reached up and lightly grazed the indentation in his left cheek—the hint that he was smiling.

Though her hand trembled, all her fear had evaporated into the void. Hopeful anticipation coursed through her veins, flooding her with warmth.

No longer fighting the current, she longed to see where it would take her.

Colt released a soft groan as she wove her fingers through his hair, gently tugging his head toward hers.

When his lips captured her mouth, the walls around her heart collapsed into a thousand grains of sand.

⭐

*C*olt thought he knew what it meant to live his life to the fullest.

But kissing Penny, he realized he hadn't even scratched the surface... until now.

She tasted sweeter than a chocolate éclair and more satisfying than a five-course meal at his favorite restaurant in Paris. And now that he'd whet his appetite, nothing else would suffice.

He had only one choice to keep the promise he'd made to his father *and* the woman who'd captured his heart—convince Penny to travel the world with him. A feat that seemed more and more attainable by the second.

When they finally broke apart, breathless and panting, Colt couldn't wait to get lost in her lips again. Who needed air? He was fairly confident he could live off her affection forever.

"What just happened?" Her breath ragged and hoarse, she sounded surprised but nowhere near displeased—thank goodness.

Not that he should worry. This kiss *had* been her idea. Even though he'd most certainly been thinking about it. And unwittingly made it possible thanks to his bonehead mistake with the batteries. He'd have to commend his subconscious mind for planning ahead.

"I don't know," he admitted, his throat equally thick. "But I wouldn't mind trying it again."

She giggled softly, sending his pulse into overdrive.

His fingers knowing exactly where to go in the darkness, gently cupped her chin, tilting her face as he lowered his mouth to hers once more.

But a sudden burst of light shattered the moment.

"Sorry, bro." A college-aged kid with absurdly large biceps wore an impish grin as he leered at Penny. "Didn't mean to interrupt."

His equally fit friend emerged from the tunnel behind him, bumping into his broad back. "Move, man. You're blocking the exit."

Sidestepping out of the way, Leering Guy hooked his thumb in their direction. Wiggling his eyebrows, he jeered, "They should've put a sock on the stalagmite."

They shared a boorish chortle.

Penny flushed, igniting Colt's protective instinct. "Hey, *bro*,"—he coated the word with an extra dose of disdain—"our headlamps went out. We were waiting for the next group to catch up and lead the way to the Concert Hall."

Okay, so a tiny lie. But they *would* need light to get out of here. He just hadn't been in a hurry until now.

"No prob, dude. We've got you covered." Bro Number Two flashed an unctuous smile at Penny as though she was supposed to be impressed.

As she inched closer, Colt draped a shielding arm around her shoulder. If these guys weren't careful, they'd get a fist to their chiseled jaws.

Fortunately, they made it the short distance to the last cave without a brawl, but Colt made sure they separated as quickly as possible once they joined the rest of the group.

The Concert Hall was the largest cavern on the tour and got its name, in part, from the unusual rock formation that resembled long pews carved into the wall. Even more impressive, the unconventional seating faced a small underground lake illuminated by strategically placed artificial lighting.

"Oh, my..." Penny breathed by his side.

Catching the beguiling look of pure wonder sprawled across her face, he resisted the urge to kiss her right there in front of everyone. Seeing the world through her eyes added a new dimension to everything, creating a deeper, more meaningful experience, as though his vision had transformed from black-and-white to color for the first time.

"Pretty cool, huh?"

"It's magical."

"Just wait. You haven't seen the best part." Placing a hand on her lower back—an area his fingertips longed to explore further—he guided her toward one of the pews. The rest of the group, including those in Brian's party, sat with bated breath, eager for the grand finale of the tour.

After Martin arrived with the last couple, he gave a brief introduction before asking everyone to turn off their headlamps.

A hush settled over the crowd as the lake became the only visible sight.

Knowing what would come next, Colt watched Penny, mesmerized by the way her eyes widened and her lips parted ever so slightly as ethereal music flooded the cavern, reverberating off the limestone walls.

She gasped as a large raft appeared around a distant corner, ferrying four musicians across the still water that shimmered like liquid emeralds. "I don't believe what I'm seeing," she purred softly. "Are they playing a cello and a violin? And is that... a *piano?*"

"A harpsichord, actually," Colt explained in a hushed voice.

"It's stunning. I've heard Beethoven's 'Moonlight Sonata' before, but never like this."

"I've only seen this one other time. At Cuevas del Drach in Palma de Mallorca, Spain. They played 'Barcarollé from *Les Contes d'Hoffmann* and it was hauntingly beautiful."

"You've seen a lot of incredible things, haven't you?"

Although she spoke barely above a whisper, her tone fluttered with curiosity.

"I have." He paused, gathering a breath of courage before murmuring, "There's so much I could show you."

For a long moment, she didn't respond, and Colt waited in agony, wishing he could see her face more clearly—to glimpse some small clue to gauge her reaction.

Finally, she whispered, "I'd like that."

Even as the crescendo swelled, filling the cavern with a soul-stirring melody, Colt had never heard a more beautiful sound than those three words.

And he wanted to savor them for as long as possible.

CHAPTER 19

"*H*e kissed you?" Eliza squealed before clamping a hand over her mouth.

"Shh," Penny hissed, glancing over her shoulder to make sure no one overheard them—especially Colt.

He stood on the far end of the town square in a huddle with the other guys, gawking as Jack tried to stuff an entire meatball sub in his mouth, presumably on a bet.

Whipping back around to Cassie and Eliza's refreshment stand, Penny lowered her voice. "*Technically*, I kissed him."

"I don't believe it!" Eliza's huge chocolate eyes mirrored her disbelief.

"He's totally smitten." Cassie grinned as she watched her brother-in-law steal a glance in their direction, then abruptly look away when he got caught.

Penny blushed. "Maybe. I don't know."

"What do you mean you don't—" Eliza snapped her mouth shut as Dolores Whittaker strolled toward them, the gentle breeze ruffling her bouffant of white curls.

"Pleasant evening, isn't it?" Dolores's kind eyes sparkled behind her Coke-bottle glasses as she lifted a small plate from the towering stack. "Your mother couldn't have asked for better weather."

"True," Eliza agreed with a smile. "But you know how she is… the show would go on in the middle of a hurricane."

The women shared a good-natured laugh.

Sylvia Carter, a former Broadway actress turned amateur director, was well known around town for her low-budget, high-energy performances—the most notable being her one-night-only Shakespeare in the Park extravaganza. Each year, she chose a different Shakespearean play, but reworked the familiar story around an unexpected setting. Local vendors like The Calendar Café and Buttercup Bistro would craft delicious foods around the unusual theme.

This year, they would perform *Romeo and Juliet*. But instead of the Renaissance era, the tragic love story would take place in twenty-first century Little Italy between two rival Italian restaurants—each claiming to have the best meatball subs in Manhattan. Which Penny found ironic considering the sandwich wasn't even Italian.

"What's on the dessert menu, ladies?" Dolores asked, eyeing the delectable spread of Italian pastries.

"Cannoli, pizzelle, sfogliatella, and of course, mini tiramisu cheesecakes." Eliza beamed proudly.

"Oh, I'll take one of those, please."

As Eliza slid the tiny treat on Dolores's plate, Cassie asked, "What would you like to drink? We have water, herbal iced tea, and a robust Italian roast."

"If tonight is anything like last year's performance, I'd better take the Italian roast if I want to stay awake until the final curtain call."

Penny choked back a giggle. Last year, Bill Tucker was supposed to play Hamlet, but his mare, Winnie, went into labor an hour before the show. So Sylvia wound up playing Hamlet in addition to her own parts. Needless to say, the extra costume changes alone added several minutes. Plus, Sylvia would run from one end of the stage to the next each time she switched roles. But in the end, it wound up being one of the most entertaining shows in Poppy Creek's history.

"Thank you, dear," Dolores told Cassie as she balanced the to-go cup on the edge of her plate. Turning to Penny, she added, "Don't look now, but a certain gentleman keeps glancing this way. And I don't think he's staring at the cannoli."

With a twinkle in her eye, she spun on her orthopedic shoes and meandered toward the crescent-shaped arrangement of folding chairs in front of the makeshift stage.

Penny's cheeks flushed as red as the raspberries adorning the mini cheesecakes.

"See?" Eliza grinned. "Everyone can tell he likes you. Why are you still fighting it?"

"Because..." Penny trailed off, toying with the tie on her vintage wrap dress. "It's Colt."

"And?" Eliza pressed. "He's clearly not the same irresponsible commitaphobe he used to be."

"And you clearly have feelings for him, too," Cassie added softly.

Penny cinched her waistline so tight, she struggled to breathe. Loosening the knot, she released a deep, uncertain breath. "But what if he hasn't really changed? What if it's—"

"An act?" Eliza asked bluntly.

Penny nodded, feeling nauseous at the thought.

"I suppose it's possible," Eliza admitted. "But it's not likely. Besides, at some point, you have to decide if you're going to trust someone or not. Like with Grant's mother. After everything she put me through, I have no reason to give her a second chance. But I honestly think she regrets her actions. And while there are times when I wrestle with bitterness, I choose to believe she wants to make things right. And I'm willing to try."

Moved by Eliza's admission, Penny wanted to throw her arms

around her friend and hug her tightly for being so brave. Harriet Parker's transgression would be deemed unforgivable by many. After all, she'd blackmailed Eliza into keeping Ben a secret from Grant, robbing them of over seven years of being a family. But the way both Eliza and Grant had chosen compassion over hate painted a beautiful picture of the healing power of forgiveness.

And she longed to have that much strength.

"What does Colt have to say about all of this?" Cassie asked.

"That's the thing… we haven't really talked about it. We had a magical evening, then when it came time to say goodbye, he got… I don't know… *shy*, almost. Which isn't like Colt."

"It certainly isn't!" Eliza agreed.

"It's sweet." Cassie pressed a hand to her heart, a dreamy smile accentuating her pretty features.

"It's confusing, is what it is," Penny sighed. "I just wish I knew what he was thinking. But he's been helping Frank roast all day, and I've been watching the shop since it's Bree's day off. This is the first time I've seen him since last night."

Cassie cast a hopeful glance in Colt's direction. "Maybe tonight you'll get your chance."

Penny followed her gaze, her stomach churning. More than anything, she wanted to believe he'd changed. After all, he'd proven himself to be beyond reliable, even to the point of risking his own life to protect her.

Why couldn't she let go of her fears?

Colt Davis wasn't her mother.

Or Lance Ferris.

※

*O*nce again, the girls had caught him staring in their direction. Colt quickly looked away, trying his best to focus on Reed's gardening-related anecdote about pill bugs being crustaceans rather than insects.

But even if he'd found the topic of conversation remotely interesting, he'd find it difficult to concentrate. He hadn't stopped thinking about Penny all day. Or their life-altering kiss. In fact, he'd almost burned down Frank's barn when he forgot to turn off the roasting machine. It had maxed out at six hundred degrees, completely scorching the entire roast, much to Frank's annoyance.

Considering he'd fried the first batch of coffee he'd been allowed to roast by himself, Colt didn't think he'd get to design his own blend anytime soon.

"Hey! Davis!" Jack waved his burly hand in front of Colt's face, startling him to attention. "For someone who has zero interest in Penny Heart, you're staring at her like she's the last rib on the platter."

Colt cleared his throat. "Yeah, well... I wouldn't say I have *zero* interest."

"Gee, no kidding." Jack rolled his eyes.

"Don't tell me we've lost you, too." Incredulous, Reed shook his head. "I thought you'd be the last bachelor standing. Now, it's between me and Jack."

"Don't be so sure," Jack laughed. "Colt had to fall for the one woman immune to his roguish charms."

"Not completely immune," Colt mumbled, his cheeks heated.

"What?" Luke cried in shock, spewing a mouthful of coffee into the grass. "Are you dating Penny? Cassie hasn't mentioned anything to me about it."

"We're not dating *exactly*." Colt shifted his feet, regretting the current topic of conversation. "I haven't asked her out yet. Officially, that is. But I plan to. Soon."

Luke frowned. "I hope you know what you're doing."

"I do." Colt held his brother's gaze.

"I think it's great," Grant cut in with a warm vote of approval. "After what happened with that Lance guy, Penny deserves some happiness. And crazy as it sounds, I think you two bring out the best in each other."

Colt immediately straightened. "What Lance guy?"

"Penny's ex." Grant blinked in surprise, repositioning his wire-frame glasses on the bridge of his nose. "I thought you knew about him."

"No." Gritting his teeth, Colt turned to Jack. "Is Lance the art dealer you told me about?"

"Maybe." Jack shrugged. "I don't remember his name."

"Yeah, that's the guy." Grant snapped his fingers in recognition. "They dated a few years ago. I overheard Eliza telling Cassie about him the other night. But I didn't get the impression it was a secret or anything."

"Did Eliza say why they broke up?" Colt asked eagerly, in dire need to learn every last detail.

"Sorry, I don't remember. I was teaching Ben to play chess while the girls talked in the kitchen. I didn't hear everything. But it sounded like Penny got her heart broken pretty badly."

Colt's hands involuntarily coiled into fists at his sides.

"Listen, Colt," Luke interjected, his tone kind but firm. "Promise me you won't pursue Penny unless you're serious about a future with her."

"Done." Colt extended his hand.

Luke hesitated a moment, eyeing his open palm warily. "Are you sure?"

"I've never been more certain about anything in my life."

And to his surprise, he actually meant it.

CHAPTER 20

*C*lutching her cup of tea, Penny stared wide-eyed as Colt strode across the lawn straight toward her. His intense, purposeful gaze sent a shiver down her spine, weakening her knees.

"Penny Heart..." He stood mere inches away, and she could see the nervous glint in his eyes as he asked, "Will you go out with me? On a proper date?"

Her lips parted, but no words escaped.

This was it—the defining moment. Whatever she said next would change everything.

She must have hesitated longer than she thought, because Eliza cleared her throat, drawing her awareness back to Colt's questioning gaze.

At the tender hopefulness in his turquoise-blue eyes, warmth radiated throughout her entire body.

The man standing before her was so different from the boy she remembered. His strength of character over the last several days had surprised her in the best possible way. And despite her fears, he'd more than earned her trust... hadn't he?

"Yes," she finally croaked, although it sounded more like a question than an answer.

Joyful relief flickered across his face. "Great! How about this Saturday at noon, if you can get Bree to cover for you?"

"Okay." She attempted a smile, hoping he couldn't detect the slight waver in her voice.

He grinned, revealing the dimple in his left cheek—the one she'd grazed with her fingertips less than twenty-four hours earlier. At the sight of it, she nearly lost her breath.

Colt opened his mouth, but before he could speak, Sylvia mounted the stage. She commanded everyone's attention in her full chef's attire, complete with a puffy white toque askew on top of her head. In her booming theater voice, she asked everyone to take a seat.

With the same endearing glimmer in his eyes as before, Colt gestured toward the folding chairs. "Would you like to...?"

Penny's throat went dry. Was he proposing they sit together? Right now? In front of everyone?

Glancing over her shoulder, she silently pleaded with Eliza and Cassie for assistance.

They merely grinned like giddy schoolgirls.

Beaming broadly, Eliza flapped her hand in an enthusiastic wave. "See you after the show."

Well, they were no help. Gathering a lungful of courage, she turned to face Colt.

"Shall we?" He offered his arm.

Digging her nails into the paper cup, she hooked her free hand through the crook in his elbow, gulping as he led her toward the back row.

Her friend, and sweet shop owner, Sadie Hamilton, raised both eyebrows in surprise as they squeezed past her. Penny could feel her curious gaze follow them as they settled onto the squeaking plastic cushions.

Is *this* what it would be like if she and Colt officially dated? Everyone in town watching their every movement with blatant interest, waiting until he disappeared on his next grand adventure, leaving her behind?

The morose thought left a sour taste in her mouth that even the sweetened iced tea couldn't squelch.

Smoothing the soft cotton folds of her dress over her knees, she tried to concentrate on the stage. *Not* on the way Colt's bare arm gently brushed against hers as he flipped through the program.

Apparently oblivious to the spark of electricity setting her skin ablaze, he chuckled under his breath. "Looks like Eliza's mom is playing Juliet *and* Friar Lawrence. Considering they're in the same scene, this should be interesting."

"It always is," she said with a shaky laugh. "But I love seeing the way she reimagines everything."

Growing up, when other kids bemoaned studying Shakespeare in school, Penny relished digging into the text, analyzing every lyrical turn of phrase. Unsurprisingly, *Romeo and Juliet* ranked highly among her favorite works of the Bard. The love story spoke to her conviction that all romances were really tragedies in a feeble disguise.

After her breakup with Lance—her first and only boyfriend —she'd watched every film version Hollywood ever made, reminding herself she'd been lucky her love story ended before the third act. In her case, she'd been on the verge of falling madly in love, but hadn't lowered all her walls quite yet. Which meant her heart wasn't completely shattered when he took the chief curator job at the Metropolitan Museum of Art, ending their blossoming relationship. But the heartbreak had been just potent enough to fortify the walls around her heart, reinforcing her long-held belief in the futility of falling in love.

Now, as she sat beside Colt, preparing to raise the curtain on their own fragile romance, she couldn't help wondering if it was doomed before it ever began.

But deep in her heart of hearts, she desperately wanted to believe he would stay.

***

*P*enny Heart had agreed to a date! And Colt knew exactly where he wanted to take her.

Whistling to himself, he skipped up the porch steps, almost bumping into Beverly as she emerged through the front door.

"My goodness, someone's in a good mood," she said with a twinkling laugh.

Colt's jubilant grin broadened.

"Either the play was exceptionally good this year or it was the company," Beverly mused.

"Let's just say, I don't remember much about the play," he chuckled. Truthfully, he'd kept stealing glances at Penny, preferring to watch her reactions than the actual performance.

"Oh, to be young and in love again," she murmured wistfully.

Noting the faint sadness in her voice, Colt asked, "How's Frank doing tonight?"

"It's tough to say," she admitted, her delicate features strained. "Physically, I'd say there's slight improvement. But..." She trailed off, as though hesitant to explain further.

"But?" he pressed gently.

"I... I can sense him pulling away. And I don't know why." Her voice cracked, and Colt placed a hand on her slender shoulder.

"Hey, I'm sure it's nothing. Men get grumpy when they aren't feeling well. It's scientifically proven that women handle physical ailments much better than we do." Okay, so he wasn't sure if that was entirely true, but it seemed to make her feel better.

"He *does* get awfully cranky when he has a cold. One little sniffle and you'd think he contracted the black plague."

"See, I wouldn't worry about it."

She smiled softly. "I'm sure you're right." Making her way toward the steps, she paused, one hand on the railing. "Oh, I almost forgot… I found Timothy Heart's obituary."

Colt's pulse spiked. "You did?"

"Yes, and it's the strangest thing." Her frown lines deepened. "It said he died in a hang glider accident. But apparently, they never found his body or the glider."

His heartbeat stuttered to a stop. *What?* He must've misheard. "Are you sure that's what it said?"

"Yes. Although, even as a head reporter turned editor-in-chief, Percy Flannigan never does his research. Once, he printed an entire article on killer butterflies that evolved to live off human flesh. It ruined the Butterfly Festival that year. And it all started when he overheard Bill and Mac discussing a B-rated horror film they saw at the drive-in." She shook her head in bemusement before adding, "When it comes to obituaries, I wouldn't be surprised if he simply asked the next of kin what happened."

As Colt mulled over her conjecture, his mind wandered to his conversation with Penny the day they went zip-lining, recalling the similarities to the childhood story told by her father. Could it simply be a strange coincidence? It seemed unlikely.

"Is something wrong?" Beverly asked. She must have noticed his uneasy expression.

"No," he said quickly. Until he knew more, he didn't want to raise any alarms. "Thanks for looking into that for me."

"Of course, dear." Her features softened. "That girl is like a daughter to me, you know. I was married once, but we never had any children of our own."

Colt blinked in surprise. He'd known Beverly his entire life, but didn't remember her ever being married.

As if reading his mind, she told him, "Harold passed away before you were born. One of the many brave men who never came home from the war."

"I'm so sorry to hear that." He studied her in the dim porch light, imagining what she must have looked like all those years ago. Her hair, though long and coiled on top of her head, shone a delicate silver now. But her eyes—a pale, periwinkle blue—still sparkled with a youthful glow. No doubt, she was a beautiful woman at any age. A wonder she never remarried in all that time.

"Harold and I were only married six months before he deployed. But in those six months, I loved deeply enough for two lifetimes. I... I never thought that would happen again." Her admission escaped on a breath so faint, Colt had to lean forward to catch it all.

"I can't imagine losing the love of your life after such a short amount of time." His chest constricted as his thoughts flew to Penny.

"It's an agony I wouldn't wish on anyone. And yet..." An unexpected smile tipped the corners of her mouth. "Every laugh we shared, every tender kiss, every moment that turned into a cherished memory, they're worth so much more than the tears I cried."

Moved by her declaration, Colt smiled past the tightness in his throat.

With a long, delicate finger, Beverly wiped an errant tear from her cheek. "Love is a gift in this life, not a guarantee. And if you're blessed to find it, you do whatever it takes to keep it. Even when it's hard."

Something about the way she looked at him led Colt to believe her words of wisdom were for his benefit. "Yes, ma'am," he said wholeheartedly.

"Good." She dipped her head in an approving nod, like a teacher who'd finally gotten through to her pupil. "Sweet dreams, dear one."

With a final goodbye, she turned and descended the porch steps, disappearing into the moonlit shadows.

As Colt watched her go, his mind churned with everything that had transpired.

And everything he needed to do next.

Including asking someone for a personal favor.

*a*s Colt hung up the phone, his heart swelled with gratitude and elated anticipation. Thanks to his unexpected ally, he'd be able to give Penny the epic first date she deserved.

Stuffing his cell in his back pocket, he pushed through the front door of Thistle & Thorn.

Glancing up from a history book laid open on the checkout counter, Bree flushed a pale pink that matched her bubblegum-colored poodle skirt. "Hi," she said with a shy smile. "Penny's not here right now."

"I know." Colt flashed a mischievous grin. He'd asked Cassie to lure her from the store for a few minutes so he could talk to Bree alone. "I'm actually looking for you."

"Y-you are?" she stammered in surprise.

"Yep." He sidestepped a large wooden butter churn and approached the counter. "You know how Penny asked you to build a sandcastle for her when you move to Santa Barbara?"

"Yeah…" She cocked her head curiously.

"For our date on Saturday, I'd like to take her somewhere to build her own. Do you know if she has a favorite beach?"

"What a great idea!" Bree beamed, before pinching her brows in contemplation. "I don't recall her ever mentioning a specific beach. But..." She trailed off, tapping a finger to her lips.

"But what?"

"Well, she has this photograph of a beach hanging in her kitchen. It stood out to me because the rest of her artwork is either a painting or a tapestry. So, the photograph seems personal, you know?"

Colt nodded, his heartbeat accelerating.

"I asked her about it,"—Bree continued with a small shrug —"but all she said was something vague about it being her happy place."

Deep in thought, Colt ran a hand through his hair. Penny's happy place sounded perfect, but how would he find out where the photograph was taken? Suddenly, an idea struck him, and he leaned across the counter eagerly. "Bree, can you do me a huge favor?"

"Maybe." She squinted through thick eyelashes. "What kind of favor?"

"I need you to stand guard while I sneak into Penny's apartment for a peek at that photo."

Her eyes widened. "Oh, I don't know..."

"I admit, it's a long shot," he said in a rush, his adrenaline pumping now. "But I have an idea. And if it works, I'm sure Penny won't mind the brief intrusion."

Chewing her bottom lip, she glanced at the front door. "But what if she comes back while you're up there?"

"I'm sure you'll think of some way to stall her. I can be in and out in less than ten minutes," he assured her.

"I guess it *would* be pretty special if you could find the same beach," Bree admitted slowly, a smile lighting her eyes. "Okay, I'll be lookout."

"Perfect! Thank you." Excitement rising in his chest, he strode toward the back of the shop.

"Wait! One more thing." Bree leveled a serious gaze on him. "Make sure you close the door behind you. The frame is warped and it won't shut all the way unless you really give it a good shove."

"I'll be in and out so quickly, I figured I'd just leave it open."

"Don't do that!" she gasped in horror. "Chip'll get out."

"Chip?"

"Penny's pet tortoise." She sounded surprised the name didn't register.

"Right, got it." He made a mental note to learn all there was to know about Penny during their date on Saturday. With the way he felt about her, he should be intimately acquainted with details like having a pet tortoise. "I'll make sure it's closed."

Satisfied, Bree turned to face the entrance, keeping her eyes peeled for Penny.

As Colt made his way through the back of the shop and up the narrow staircase, his pulse quickened. While he'd prefer not to visit Penny's apartment for the first time without her, the opportunity was too serendipitous to pass up. He only hoped his efforts paid off.

After finagling his way through the finicky front door with an exaggerated nudge, his jaw dropped. The interior of Penny's home mirrored her personality—warm, vibrant, and completely captivating—from the boho-chic style to the inviting scent of sweet tea leaves that lingered in the air. He longed to explore every inch of the enticing space, but time—and his anti-snooping conscience—kept him on track.

He needed to find the photograph.

After ensuring the front door was latched securely, he quickly scanned the walls of the tiny kitchen, finally landing on a framed photograph of two young girls building a sandcastle on the beach. *Bingo.*

Gently lifting it off the wall, he laid it facedown on the tile counter.

He froze when he heard a faint rustling of leaves.

Following the sound, he marveled as a large tortoise emerged through a thicket of house plants.

The curious animal seemed to glare at him through narrowed eyelids.

"You must be Chip. Sorry, pal. I'll be out of your hair in a second. I'm just—" He paused. Why in the world was he explaining himself to a reptile?

Exhaling a jittery laugh, he returned his attention to the task at hand.

His fingers tingled with hopeful expectation as he turned the tabs holding the backing in place. As he removed it, he flashed back to the afternoon in the storage room when Penny showed him the inscription, regaling him with the bewitching story about the woman in the picture. He could still envision the shimmer in her eyes as she discovered the hidden message.

Colt peeled back the flimsy sheet of cardboard, holding his breath as his eyes strained to locate the object of his search.

Eureka!

There, in the lower right-hand corner, he found exactly what he was looking for.

But before he could whoop in triumph, a vibration in his back pocket disrupted the moment.

Slipping out his cell phone, his heartbeat stalled at the text on the screen.

Good news! The opportunity you've been waiting for has just opened up....

*G*azing across the counter at Cassie and Eliza, Penny licked a smear of chocolate sauce off her bottom lip. "This is incredible! But what exactly am I tasting?"

"It's a chocolate peanut butter pie with a mochaccino mousse."

Eliza's dark eyes glowed with pride. "It's for the Fourth of July pie contest."

"If it were up to me, I'd give you the blue ribbon right now." Penny dug her fork into the creamy filling, eager for another bite.

"That's what I told her." Cassie smiled, turning from her copper espresso machine with a fresh latte in hand. "But she wanted a second opinion."

"Cassie loves anything with coffee in it, so she's biased," Eliza explained with a good-natured grin. "But if *you* like it, even as a non-coffee drinker, I know it's a winner."

"I love it," Penny told her sincerely. "The coffee flavor is subtle and pairs perfectly with the sweetness of the peanut butter and chocolate."

"Hooray! I'm so happy to hear that." Eliza clasped her hands together, bouncing on her toes. "I'm determined to top Frida Connelly's cinnamon pecan pie. Although, I'm pretty sure she bribes the judges since she wins every year."

"You're probably right," Penny laughed. "But this is definitely delicious enough to take first place." Savoring another bite, she mumbled, "I can't believe it's almost July. It seems like only yesterday you were a June Bride."

Cassie beamed. "I know! Time flies, doesn't it? But I'm looking forward to my first Fourth of July in Poppy Creek. Luke says after the festivities in the town square, there are fireworks at Willow Lake."

"That's my favorite part," Penny admitted, wondering what it would be like to watch the stunning display with Colt by her side. Involuntary chills ran down her spine at the thought.

"Remember Colt's last Fourth of July picnic?" Eliza snickered.

Penny groaned, wrenched from her pleasant reverie. "Don't remind me."

"What happened?" Cassie asked, glancing between them.

"Colt used to be quite the prankster," Eliza said with a bemused shake of her head. "For some reason, he thought it would be funny to set off the sprinklers in the town square. Everything got soaked, including the pie tent. No one won a blue ribbon that year."

"Oh no! That's terrible," Cassie gasped.

"People were pretty upset about it." Penny cringed at the memory. "Especially Mayor Burns. It was his first year in office." Truthfully, she'd never seen the man look so upset. "To this day, they keep all the tents off the lawn. They close off the streets to through traffic and set them up there, instead."

"Well, I'm sure Colt learned his lesson," Cassie said kindly. "I doubt he'd do something like that now."

"He's changed a lot since our childhood years," Eliza agreed. "Especially since you two started hanging out."

Penny flushed as Eliza smirked in her direction.

"To think," Eliza continued, "none of this would have happened if Cassie hadn't told Mayor Burns to pair the two of you together."

"What?" Startled, Penny darted her gaze from Eliza to Cassie. "It was *your* idea?"

Cassie's cheeks turned the same bright red as her apron. "I didn't *tell* him to, exactly. I overheard him mentioning the change he wanted to make to the article's topic. And I merely suggested Colt had a lot of experience in that area. I had no idea he'd be so excited about it. I actually got the impression he knew Colt wouldn't be thrilled, which is why he found the idea so appealing."

"That's no surprise," Eliza snorted. "He probably figured it was payback for all of Colt's antics back in high school. Little did he realize he'd be the catalyst for Colt's happily ever after."

Her friends turned affectionate gazes in her direction, and Penny shifted on the barstool.

It seemed like everyone had their future all planned out.

If only she had the same level of certainty.

CHAPTER 22

*T*he days leading up to their date passed by agonizingly slow. And now that the moment had finally arrived, Colt teetered between nervous and exhilarated.

He still couldn't get over the vision of Penny waiting to greet him on the sidewalk that afternoon, her slender figure showcased in a long, flowing dress more vibrant than the summer sun. Her striking auburn hair fell around her shoulders in soft waves, and he'd longed to run his fingers through the silky strands.

But first, they needed to arrive at their intended destination—Penny's happy place. He'd spent an entire day tracking down the right beach, and he hoped she would forgive his snooping once she realized the reason behind it.

As they zipped around winding mountain roads in Penny's Mustang, Colt regretted not having a car of his own. While they'd made leaps and bounds in the adventure department, she staunchly refused to lay a finger on his motorcycle, let alone ride on the back of it. Not that it would matter in a few weeks. If his plan came to fruition, they wouldn't need either mode of transportation.

He stole a glance at Penny in the passenger seat, noticing the way she sat up a little straighter when they reached a familiar fork in the road. When he veered to the right, she turned to gape at him in bewilderment.

"Wait. We're not headed where I think we're headed... are we?"

"You'll have to wait and see." He flashed a devilish grin, enjoying the ardent curiosity sprawled across her features.

As they approached the towering wooden archway, Penny's gaze darted from Colt to the rustic sign. "We're going back to Lupine Ridge Ranch?"

He chuckled at the incredulity in her voice.

"I mean, clearly we *are*," she said in a rush. "But why? Are we horseback riding again?"

He sensed the faint hesitation in her tone and smiled. "Nope. I called in a favor."

And if he were honest, it wasn't an easy phone call to make. Rational or not, he viewed Hunter as a rival, of sorts. And he didn't relish having to rely on him to make Penny's special day a reality. But in the end, it was well worth a blow to his pride. And once again, Hunter had proved to be a stand-up guy. Possibly even a friend, if Colt planned to stick around.

When they deviated off the main road down a dirt path, away from the lodge and stables, Penny swiftly rolled down the window, craning her neck to ascertain their exact whereabouts.

Colt parked at the end of the narrow lane, and Penny's eyes widened at the sight of Hunter standing near an enormous metal hangar. "Hunter?" She cast an uncertain glance at Colt. "What's going on?"

"You'll have to—"

"Wait and see?" she finished with a playful smirk.

"Exactly." He grinned, climbing out of the car.

"Nice ride," Hunter said by way of greeting. "Nineteen sixty-four?"

"Sixty-five, actually," Penny corrected. "My dad and I restored it together."

For a moment, he looked surprised. Then he tipped his cowboy hat in a show of respect. "You did a mighty fine job."

"Thank you." Penny returned his smile.

Heartened by the absence of his typical jealousy, Colt extended his hand. "Thanks again for letting us borrow her."

"Anytime." Hunter shook his hand warmly. "I don't get to take her up as much as I'd like."

"Take her up?" Penny repeated in confusion, glancing between them.

"My gal, Molly. She's a beauty, isn't she?" Stepping to the side, Hunter gestured toward a cobalt-blue Piper Super Cub. With its large, durable tires and sturdy frame, it had earned a reputation in the aviation community for being one of the premier bush planes. And Colt wouldn't mind owning one himself one day. If he ever settled in one place long enough.

"Wait. You mean, we're *flying*... in *that*?" Penny balked, backing up a few steps.

Hunter's forehead creased as he glanced at Colt in concern.

Prepared for her hesitation, Colt smiled calmly. "Did you know flying in a small aircraft is eighteen-point-five percent safer than driving a car?"

Her eyebrows raised a smidge. "Really?"

"Really," Colt echoed with confidence. "And when you compare the stringent level of training necessary to acquire my pilot's license versus my driver's license, you were actually in more danger with me behind the wheel of the car than in the cockpit."

This elicited a small smile. "In that case, I'm definitely driving on the way home."

"Fair enough," he chuckled. "Will that be taking place right now? Or afterward?"

She drew her bottom lip between her teeth, mulling it over.

"Well, I guess I can't argue with statistics. You said flying is eighteen-point-five percent safer?"

"Yep. And that's only counting small, private aircraft. If you include commercial flights, you're one hundred and ninety times more likely to be in a car accident than a plane crash."

She tilted her head, clearly warming up to the idea.

"So…" he drawled, offering his hand. "Are you ready to be my copilot?"

With a meaningful glance that made his pulse race, she slipped her hand in his. "Where are we going?"

"You'll have to—"

"Don't tell me." Her lips quirked. "I'll have to wait and see?"

If Hunter wasn't standing two feet away, he would have pulled her into his arms and kissed her tempting lips right then and there. Did she have any idea how deeply he'd fallen for her?

He could only hope that after today, there wouldn't be any doubt.

*

*W*hen her feet finally landed on solid ground, Penny still felt weightless, as though she'd never returned from the clouds. She had no idea the planet looked like that—a stunning patchwork of God's creation spread out before them like an inviting quilt. And to her astonishment, she hadn't experienced an inkling of fear, only awe and wonder.

But the most euphoric part of the flight? The second they crested the rugged mountaintops and the breathtaking coastline came into view, its pristine shore presenting an arresting contrast to the hypnotic expanse of cerulean waters.

For several moments, she couldn't move, lost in the bewitching beauty displayed before her. When Colt reached out and gently touched her forearm, she'd finally noticed the silent tears trailing down her cheeks. Entwining her fingers with his, she'd hoped the warmth and pressure of her palm would communicate the words her lips couldn't.

Turning to him now, with the plane tethered to the tarmac, she couldn't hold back her swelling emotions. Throwing her arms around his broad shoulders, she buried her face in his neck whispering, "Thank you, thank you," over and over. Realizing her tears had dampened his T-shirt, she pulled away, wiping the moisture from her cheeks with the back of her hand.

"I take it you like the beach," he murmured softly, the edges of his mouth curling into a tender smile.

"I've actually never been to the beach. But I've always wanted to. I… I can't believe we're here. Sort of." She grinned, then hiccupped, sniffling as she glanced around the tiny, bare-bones airport. "I assume the beach is somewhere nearby."

"It is, but…" He trailed off in confusion. "You've never been to the beach before?"

"No. Why? Is that strange? I suppose it is, since I live less than a day's drive away. I've thought about going a hundred times, but something always got in the way." If she were honest, ever since her father's death, she'd never been brave enough to venture that far from home on her own.

"It's not that." He cleared his throat. "It's just— Well, the photograph in your kitchen of the beach… your happy place. I assumed it was somewhere you'd been before."

Her head jerked up in surprise. "When did you see that photo?"

His Adam's apple bobbed as he swallowed, a sheepish expression shadowing his features. "I wanted to take you to the beach for our first date, and when Bree told me about the photograph, it sounded perfect. So, I… stole a peek to look for an inscription. And sure enough, 'Starcross Cove' was scribbled on the back. I spent an entire day scouring the internet to find the exact beach, made a dozen or so phone calls, and… here we are." A worry wrinkle appeared in his forehead. "I'm sorry if what I did crossed a line. It was never my intention to make you uncomfortable. And I promise, I went in and out of your apartment as quickly as possible. And I—"

Penny's heartbeat thrummed so loud, the rest of Colt's confession faded into the background. Overcome with emotion, she couldn't breathe, let alone formulate a coherent response.

Colt had found the beach—*her* beach. And he'd remembered the trick about the hidden inscription. Why hadn't she ever thought to look for it? She supposed she took for granted that every photograph or painting procured by her father, he'd already checked.

Penny focused her gaze on Colt's face, her pulse fluttering at the anxious glint in his eyes.

"Pen, I'm so sorry. I—"

Popping onto her tiptoes, she curtailed his apology with a heart-stopping kiss—the kind that left her knees weak and quivering.

He hadn't just given her the perfect date. He'd given her the world. And it meant more to her than words could ever express. Hopefully, a kiss could come close.

When their lips finally parted, he released a deep and satisfied sigh, lightly resting his forehead against hers.

Brushing her fingertips across his left cheek, she murmured, "Let's go see this beach."

CHAPTER 23

*a*s Penny dug her toes into the warm grains of sand, she was struck by an odd sensation, as though the sights and sounds were at once new and strangely familiar. Almost as if she knew the salty sea breeze would carry a hint of freshly baked sourdough. And the symphony of the seagulls and soothing whisper of the surf echoed through her like a childhood lullaby.

Her chest rising and falling with the graceful undulation of each wave, she struggled to gain a foothold in her surreal surroundings.

She was here, standing on her beach. It still didn't seem possible.

The stately home on top of the hill looked exactly the same as the photograph, down to the white picket fence and pristine hedges. Her gaze traveled beyond the latched gate, along the meandering pathway to the shore until it fell upon a quilt draped across the sand. Anchored by a picnic basket and a colorful assortment of plastic buckets and shovels, it seemed to beckon her closer. Nearby, a circle of river rock formed a simple firepit, with a pile of driftwood waiting to be lit.

She turned to Colt, her eyes questioning.

"One of the calls I made yesterday was to the owner of that house." He nodded toward the home that had occupied her youthful imagination. "It's actually a women's shelter. The owner was very gracious, and when I explained my request to spend a few hours on the beach, she was eager to help. All she asked in return was that I made a donation to the shelter."

"That's so kind," she murmured, in complete awe.

"It turns out, this town has a bit of a reputation for bringing star-crossed lovers together," he said with a playful grin.

"Oh, is that what we are?" she asked with a teasing lilt, taking a step toward him. "Like Romeo and Juliet?"

He matched her step with two, his dimple on full display. "Exactly. Just replace feuding families with a few ill-timed pranks."

"A few?" she laughed.

"Okay, maybe more than a few. But who's counting?"

They stood toe to toe, and with his sunglasses poised on top of his head, she could see the laughter in his eyes. But as the sun set behind him, the sparkle in the deep pools of blue softened to a tender glimmer.

She shivered as his fingers curled around a wind-tossed strand of hair, gently sweeping it behind her ear. His hand lingered on the side of her face, his thumb caressing her cheekbone, leaving a trail of tingling heat across her skin.

"When I came home for Luke's wedding, I had no idea how my life would change." The husky timbre of his voice rippled through her, scattering goose bumps down her arms. "And now, I only seem to know one thing for certain. Penny Heart, I have fallen so deeply in love with you, I can't see a way out. And I don't want one. Without you, Everest is just another mountain. And the Grand Canyon? A hole in the ground."

Joy bubbling to the surface, she beamed up at him through happy tears. "It's descriptions like those that got you out of writing the guidebook article," she teased, though her voice was thick with emotion.

He chuckled a low, gravelly rumble as he slipped his arm around her waist.

She inhaled sharply, anticipating the warm, welcome pressure of his lips on hers.

"It's comments like that one that will get you a dip in the ocean." In one fell swoop, he hoisted her over his shoulder.

Laughing breathlessly, she made a show of fighting him off.

But deep down, she hoped he never let her go.

Colt Davis had said he loved her!

And even more unexpected…

Was how badly she wanted to say it back.

*

*N*o matter how many times Colt tried to focus on the sun slipping behind the horizon, casting streaks of gold, amber, and magenta across the dusky blue water, he couldn't. Not with Penny curled up beside him, her head resting on his chest.

His heart had never been as full as when he'd watched her frolic in the gentle surf, kicking up sprays of water like confetti. And later, when they'd built the sandcastle that now stood proudly by their feet, she'd worn an expression of such pure and unbridled joy, the beauty of it made his chest ache.

But the best part? The stolen glances she'd cast in his direction as they'd knelt side by side in the sand. While she hadn't returned his declaration of love in so many words, she'd done so with the soulful shimmer in her eyes, the flush of her cheeks, and each earth-shattering kiss. And he would wait as long as he needed to in order to hear the soul-affirming phrase spill from her lips.

The modest campfire crackled as night fell upon them and the sky traded a myriad of vivid colors for a canopy of stars.

Penny snuggled closer. "Does this mean we have to go soon? I imagine it's difficult to fly in the dark."

He smiled at the wistful sigh that accompanied her question. "I've logged plenty of night flights over the years. And I made sure the trolley taking us back to the airport runs late enough. There's something else I want to show you before we leave."

"There's more? Why, Mr. Davis... you spoil me."

His chest swelled at the laughter in her voice, and he kissed the top of her head, taking a moment to savor the sweet scent of her floral shampoo mixed with the crisp, salty air. "That's the idea. Keep an eye on the water."

Relishing the weight of Penny nestled in his arms, Colt held his breath, utilizing every fiber of his being to take a mental picture, praying it would last forever. While many more adventures awaited them, some moments surpassed the rest—a snapshot of a perfect point in time.

Penny's soft gasp drew his attention to the waves tumbling toward the shore. Lit from within, the dark indigo surface shone an electric blue as though someone held a neon sign beneath the water.

"What is it?" she breathed.

"They're bioluminescent waves. The phenomenon is caused by phytoplankton."

"It's breathtaking. Like something out of a fairy tale."

"It happens all along the California coast, but rarely ever in the same place at the same time. But for some reason, it occurs every summer in Starcross Cove. Legend has it, hundreds of years ago, two shooting stars crossed paths in the night sky, collided, and crashed into the sea, dispersing their light below the surface of the water... and their magic."

"Magic?" She tilted her chin to gaze up him, and for a

moment, his heart stopped at the look of wonder in her luminous eyes.

"According to the legend,"—he continued, a smile on his lips—"on nights you can see the blue glow, two star-crossed lovers will be brought together."

"That's beautiful," she whispered, leaning her head back against his chest.

"The beaches are usually filled with tourists every summer, but this cove is secluded. Technically, it's shared between Starcross and its sister city, Green Castle Bay."

Penny stiffened.

Searching her expression in the firelight, his heartbeat faltered at the look of shock and distress blazed across her features. "What is it?" he asked, instantly on high alert.

"What did you say the other town was called?"

"Green Castle Bay. Why?"

She closed her eyes, pain evident in the deepened creases etched into her brow.

He shifted to get a better glimpse of her face. "Pen, you're starting to worry me. What's wrong?"

"It's..." She trailed off, her eyes shimmering with unshed tears. Finally, she whispered, "That's where my father died."

Time seemed to slow down as Colt struggled to grasp her words. "I don't understand. He died in Green Castle Bay?"

She sat up and brought her knees to her chest, staring blankly into the flickering flames. "Nine years ago, when I was away at college, I got a phone call from a complete stranger. A detective named Harold Nelson Shaw, a name I'll never forget." Her voice broke, and Colt leaned forward, placing a comforting hand on her shoulder. "They'd found my father... alone in a motel room. He'd died in his sleep. A brain aneurysm, according to the autopsy."

A single tear rolled down her cheek, and she didn't bother wiping it away. "I told them they had to be mistaken. My father never left Poppy Creek. It didn't make sense he would be so far from home. But they'd found a ticket to an antiques show in his wallet."

"Pen, I'm so sorry. Did you—"

"Have to identify the body?" She shook her head, drawing her knees in closer. "It's not like it is in movies. They used his ID and fingerprints. And he'd stipulated in his will that his viable organs would be donated, while the rest would be given to medical research."

Colt blinked, still wrapping his head around her story. "I'm sorry, Pen. I still don't fully understand. Why all the different stories about how he died?" He didn't mention what he'd learned from Beverly, deciding to be patient and hear the rest of her explanation.

More tears followed the first, and for a moment, she buried her face in her hands, unable to speak.

His gut wrenching, he gently caressed her back, giving her the time she needed.

Sniffling, she stretched out her legs and turned to face him. "I know it sounds awful, but…" She hesitated, her breath faltering.

He reached for her hand, giving it a squeeze.

Inhaling deeply, she dried her eyes with the tip of her finger. "I couldn't bear to have his life end like that, for that to be the last thing people remembered about him… the last thing *I* remembered." Her lower lip trembled as she pressed on, fighting back tears. "It wasn't a secret that people thought my father was odd. A timid, reclusive man who owned the strange store in town and rarely ventured beyond his front door. But that's not how I saw him. My dad was the most adventurous man alive, with a vibrant, colorful imagination and a heart as brave and bold as the sea. I know it sounds foolish, but I suppose I wanted everyone to remember him the way I did. Not as a sad, fearful man who died alone in a motel room."

The last word escaped on a sob, and as her shoulders shook,

Colt wrapped his arms around her, pulling her against him. He stroked her hair as she cried softly.

"I planned to tell the truth eventually, I just... I couldn't," she confessed in a hoarse whisper. "But I shouldn't have lied to everyone."

"How about we call it a legend instead?"

"A legend?" she echoed, a subtle shift in her breathing—steadier than before. "I like that."

Curling into him, she gazed out at the incandescent waves. After a long pause, she murmured, "You know, some legends are actually true."

"Any one in particular come to mind?" His heartbeat raced with unrestrained hope.

"Take Starcross Cove for example." She shifted position in order to face him, a bewitching glimmer in her eyes. "And us. Do you know any two people less likely to fall in love than you and me?"

His breathing stalled, leaving him a little lightheaded. "Is that what we are? Two people in love?"

A coy smile tipped the edges of her lips as she said, "'My bounty is as boundless as the sea, my love as deep; the more I give to thee, the more I have, for both are infinite.'"

Recognizing Juliet's lines from Shakespeare's *Romeo and Juliet*, Colt hungrily captured her mouth with his.

Never in all his life, had he flown so high.

And he hoped he never came back down.

CHAPTER 24

The slow, lingering kiss beneath the flickering lamp on Main Street proved to be the perfect end to their perfect evening. And Penny couldn't help but smile as they stalled, unwilling to say good night.

In the course of a single day, their lives had completely transformed—entwined by the bonds of love, like two paths merging in the woods, becoming one road to the same destination. And as they embarked on this new journey together, Penny reveled in the exhilaration. She'd never been more excited about the future.

Colt held both of her hands, his gaze drinking her in. "There's something I've been dying to tell you all night, but the opportunity never came up."

"Oh?" she murmured, unable to fathom what else was left to say after all they'd shared.

"The other day, an old friend contacted me out of the blue." His voice rose with nervous energy, causing Penny's heartbeat to flutter with apprehension. "He runs a luxury scuba diving outfit in the Maldives, and I've been pestering him for years to set up a sister operation in the Mediterranean, hiring me as a guide since I know those waters better than anyone."

As he spoke, Penny's blood ran cold.

"Well," Colt continued, running his thumbs in small circles against her palms. "He finally got his investment partners to go for it. And they want me to fly out in two weeks."

"What?" Penny gave a small shake of her head. Surely, she'd heard him incorrectly. "I don't understand what you're saying."

"This is an unbelievable opportunity and—"

As though she'd been burned, Penny yanked her hands from his grasp, shock and dismay crashing over her. "Please tell me this is one of your pranks. You're not actually considering the job offer?"

Surprise flickered across his face. "Pen, I—"

"You already took the job, didn't you?" Her voice escaped in a hollow whisper, sudden tears burning her eyes as the harsh reality sunk in. "How could you do this? Now? After everything that's happened between us?"

Her rib cage compressed around her lungs, making it difficult to breathe. *This isn't real... this isn't real....* She recited the silent mantra, praying it was all a bad dream.

But it wasn't. She could see the truth reflected in his eyes, and she couldn't bear it any longer. Desperately, she twisted away from him, but he grabbed her hand, whirling her back around.

"Wait. I didn't finish." He pinned her with an earnest, pleading gaze. "I want you to come with me."

His words hung between them, fluttering in the wind like a white flag.

But all she saw was red.

"Come with you?" she cried, wrestling free from his hold. "For how long?"

"I don't know. Six months. Maybe more. I already told them unless you were a part of the deal, I'd turn down their offer. You'd get your own accommodations, paid travel expenses, you name it. We'll get to explore the Mediterranean Sea together. Just think of the adventures."

"Just *think*?" she blurted, bitter disappointment curling around her heart. "All I can do is think. About leaving my livelihood, Chip, my friends… my whole life is here. How can you ask me to leave it all behind for an indeterminate amount of time? With only two weeks' notice?"

She bit her bottom lip sharply, the lump in her throat swelling. How had she been so blind? She'd put her trust in this man, believing he'd changed. But all this time, he couldn't wait to leave, to go on his next big adventure. And the fact that he thought she could simply uproot her entire life to go with him— He hadn't matured at all.

"I understand it's a big ask…" He trailed off, running his fingers through his hair, his features strained in the dim light. "But I thought—"

"That's the problem," she cut in, her throat closing around her words as her anguish mounted. "You're the only one *not* thinking. You never do. You do exactly what you want, when you want. Regardless of the consequences. I'm not like you, Colt. I can't leave people behind as easily as you do."

He flinched as though he'd been slapped.

A brief pang of remorse shot through her, but she'd gone too far to turn back. She'd given him her heart, and she felt the sharp, shattered fragments pierce her chest each time she tried to breathe.

"Stay." The plea escaped in a desperate gasp before the thought had fully formed in her mind. "Please, Colt. Stay here. With me."

A dark shadow passed over his features, and when his lips finally parted, each syllable seemed to cause him physical pain. "I can't."

"Can't? Or won't?"

The answer loomed in his tortured gaze.

"I guess there's nothing else to say." Tears blurring her vision, she turned away from him, suddenly overcome with blinding anger at her own foolishness.

The image of her father on the balcony sprang from her subconscious, and all at once, she felt as though she'd let him down. He'd spent his entire life teaching her to be safe, protecting her from pain. Despite everything, she'd thrown caution to the wind, hoping she could fly.

And look how far she'd fallen.

⭐

*W*hen Colt arrived at Frank's, he sat in the driveway with his motorcycle idling, still in shock.

His perfect state of bliss had devolved into a nightmare in three seconds flat, and he could only blame himself. To make matters worse, he had no idea how to fix it. What he'd thought would be received as a romantic gesture had torn them apart. And before he'd gathered the courage to explain *why* he couldn't stay, she'd deserted him on the street corner.

Yanking off his helmet, Colt took a deep breath, but with each inhale, a sharp, throbbing pain tore through his chest. And to his surprise, a tingling, burning sensation pricked the backs of his eyes.

He'd only ever cried twice in his adult life. Once when his father was diagnosed with cancer and again when the cancer took his father's life.

Fighting with his emotions, he shifted his gaze to the car beside him, blinking a few times as he tried to register the unfamiliar vehicle. The dark-blue sedan didn't look anything like Beverly's Volvo. And the young, attractive woman exiting the front door certainly wasn't Beverly, either.

He killed the ignition before sliding off the bike.

"You must be Colt," she said, more a statement than a question.

"I am." His gaze fell to the black leather bag in her hand, and his stomach clenched. "And you are?"

"Doctor Rose Delaney."

He'd never heard of her before. She must be new in town, but Colt wasn't in the right frame of mind for pleasantries. "Is Frank okay?"

She frowned, as though trying to formulate an appropriate response. "He fell and dislocated his right shoulder. He's in considerable pain, but there's no permanent damage."

His blood pumping in alarm, Colt strode toward the porch steps, but as he maneuvered past her, she placed a gentle hand on his arm. "He'll be fine, but he needs rest. I'll come by and check on him tomorrow afternoon."

Colt nodded, gritting his teeth against the weight of helplessness pressing down on him. He was supposed to protect Frank, to keep something like this from happening. "Is Beverly here?" He scanned the driveway for her car. She'd planned to be with Frank most of the evening while he was out with Penny.

"Frank was the only one home when I arrived. I asked if I should notify a family member on his behalf, but he declined, explaining that you would be home soon. I left my cell number in case you need anything and I'm not in the office."

"Thank you. Is it okay if I see him?"

"Of course. Just know that he's... um, not in the best mood," she said ruefully.

"That doesn't surprise me. But you get used to it." He offered what he hoped was a friendly smile. Or, at least, the best he could muster under the circumstances.

After bidding her good night, he stole quietly down the hallway toward Frank's room. Frank lay in bed, his head propped up with several pillows, his arm in a sling. A small rabbit-eared TV blared on the nightstand, but he didn't appear to be watching.

"Knock, knock." Colt entered the room cautiously.

Frank grunted, staring up at the ceiling.

"I'm so sorry, Frank. I caught Dr. Delaney on her way out and she explained what happened. Can I get you anything?"

"A new body. I wouldn't mind having one like Sean Connery's in the Bond films."

Colt cracked a slight grin. At least Frank's sense of humor was still intact. "Want me to call Beverly?" Although late in the evening, he knew she would want to know what happened.

Frank's features darkened. "No. Don't bother her."

"I'm sure it's not a bother." Colt pondered how he'd feel if something happened to Penny and no one told him. Fueled by the distressing thought, he pressed on, despite Frank's insistence. "She cares about you. I really think one of us should call her."

"I didn't ask for your opinion," Frank barked.

In the back of his mind, Colt could hear his mother's voice kindly pointing out that Frank had a rough night and was in a lot of pain. Even Dr. Delaney had told him Frank needed rest. And yet, deep in his core, Colt couldn't let the topic drop. Not like this.

He kept thinking about what Beverly told him the night they crossed paths on the front porch. *Love is a gift in this life, not a guarantee. And if you're blessed to find it, you do whatever it takes to keep it. Even when it's hard.*

He'd messed things up with Penny. The damage might even be irreparable. But Frank? He still had a chance to make things work.

Squaring his shoulders, he said evenly, "Maybe not. But I'm going to give it to you, anyway. It's time to man up and quit being such a blonde roast."

Frank's eyebrows lowered. "What did you say?"

"You heard me." Colt took a deep breath, pushing forward. "You're either all in or you're out."

Frank looked away. "You don't know what you're talking about."

"Sure I do. Pursuing a woman is the same as roasting coffee.

You shouldn't do it at all if you're not going to do it right. You have a good woman, Frank. It's time you stop pushing her away."

"It's for her own good." Frank's words escaped in a low, guttural growl, and Colt was surprised by the flicker of despair in his steel-gray eyes.

"What do you mean?"

"I'm protecting her from this." Frank waved a hand over his afflicted body. "I'm a ticking time bomb, slowly counting down the seconds. Although, not as slowly as I'd like."

"It's not as bad as all that," Colt assured him quickly.

Frank met his gaze with a stone-cold stare. "Isn't it? You think I don't know why you're really here?"

Taken aback, Colt stammered, "Cassie said—"

"I know what she said. That girl is too meddlesome for her own good," he grumbled, although his tone softened with uncharacteristic affection.

"So…" Colt trailed off, putting the pieces together. "All this time, you've resented me being here?"

"I—" Frank paused, as if refraining from his usual bluntness. Finally, he murmured, "I resented *needing* you here. Which proves my point. What do I have to offer Beverly? I can't even live in my own house without a babysitter." A bitter resignation stole across his features. "I'd thought I'd been given another chance. But the heart attack made me realize I might not have much time left. She's already lost someone she loved. I won't let her go through that again."

Flooded with compassion, Colt studied the older man, noticing the angst etched into each weathered wrinkle and crease. "But what if you're wrong?" he asked gently. "Shouldn't *she* be the one who gets to decide that?"

Frank glowered, but Colt persisted.

"What if the roles were reversed? Would *you* walk away? Or would you cherish whatever time you were given regardless of what came next?"

Frank's eyes widened a fraction of a centimeter, as though Colt's words resonated on some level deep within him.

And for a moment, Colt saw a glimmer of hope....

For both of them.

CHAPTER 25

*A*part from when her father died, Penny had never experienced such soul-rending agony. Her raw throat burned from hours of sobbing, and the early morning sunlight filtering through the tall windows stung her swollen eyes.

If she could help it, she'd never leave her apartment again. Her thoughts flew to the last remaining task on the list. If she went through with it, she'd have to face Colt at the Fourth of July Festival. And she didn't think she'd survive the encounter. In fact, she wasn't sure how she'd endure the next two weeks if he decided to stay in town before catching his flight. Simply knowing he inhabited the same square mile made her heart ache.

Throwing back the covers, she swung her feet over the edge of the bed. Every muscle in her body groaned as though she'd run a marathon the day before. When people described a broken heart, they failed to mention how every fiber in your being disintegrated at the same time.

After setting the teakettle on the stove, Penny pulled a bundle of collard greens from the fridge. While she would surely never eat again, Chip shouldn't have to suffer with her. She tore off a handful, still baffled Colt presumed she could leave her life behind for six months, and maybe even longer.

Sprinkling the shredded leaves on the floor, she knelt on the carpet, waiting for Chip to emerge from his enclosure. The day she'd found him huddled in the corner of an old steamer trunk her heart had finally started to heal after her father's death.

The poor discarded pet, with his fearful eyes and chipped shell, became her family, providing a renewed sense of purpose. And caring for him had helped her recognize her own feelings of abandonment.

When Chip didn't appear, Penny rustled the leafy greens between her fingers. "Rise and shine. It's time for breakfast."

After not garnering a response, she looked inside the enclosure, brushing aside the lush foliage of surrounding houseplants.

But Chip was nowhere to be seen.

Though uncommon, he sometimes fell asleep elsewhere in the apartment. But a slice of juicy watermelon would always entice him from his hiding place.

Penny arranged a few cubes on a plate before setting it on the floor. When he still didn't surface after several minutes, panic gripped her.

A cold feeling of dread slipped down her spine as she turned toward the front door.

It hung ajar.

In her blind anguish the night before, she must have left it open.

Darting across the room, she halted at the top of the landing, peering down the dimly lit staircase. He couldn't have gone far, could he?

Grief and guilt churned inside her stomach as she scrambled down the steps into the storage room. "Chip? Chip?" She couldn't hide the terrified tremor in her voice, but she tried her best to remain outwardly calm. He had to be in here somewhere.

That's when she noticed the brocade curtain separating the

storage room from the main part of the shop had been tied back with the tasseled drapery cord.

No... She'd completely forgotten Bree volunteered to arrive early in order to receive a special delivery. A man from Sacramento had called yesterday and asked to drop off any unwanted items from his late grandfather's estate before heading back to the city.

"Bree?" Rushing into the store, Penny scanned the cluttered hardwood floor for any sign of Chip.

"Yeah?" Her helpful employee poked her head above the large cardboard box clutched in her arms.

Penny froze, watching in horror as Bree strolled through the front entrance, which she'd propped open with an old-fashioned milk can. "H-how long has the door been open?"

"I don't know. Twenty or thirty minutes, maybe?" Bree grunted as she slid the heavy box onto the table where she'd already stacked several others. "You know, I thought the guy would help me unload everything. But he simply dumped it on the sidewalk and took off. Can you believe it?"

Suddenly light-headed, Penny pressed a palm to her forehead.

"Are you okay?" Bree squinted in concern. "You look pale. And your eyes are red and puffy."

"Close the door, please." Penny leaned against the checkout counter, trying to steady her ragged breaths. She needed to get her emotions under control. Even with the door wide open, and the fact that tortoises could move quicker than most people thought, the odds were in her favor that Chip was still in the store somewhere.

After casting a worried glance over her shoulder, Bree dragged the milk can out of the way and swung the door shut. The bell twinkled cheerfully as though Penny's world wasn't crashing down around her. "What's going on?" Bree's tone carried an uncertain waver. "There are still a few boxes outside. Should I get them?"

"No." With her fingertips resting against her temple, Penny shook her head. "I need your help with something."

"Anything," Bree said quickly.

"We need to find Chip. If we don't..." Her voice cracked.

She couldn't even think about the alternative.

He was all she had left.

*A*s Colt stared at the sparkling pink stone set in the diamond-encrusted rose gold band, the knife in his heart twisted.

"What do you guys think?" Beaming proudly, Grant held up the engagement ring, turning it slowly so the late afternoon sunlight bounced off each meticulously cut gem.

While Luke, Jack, and Reed commended Grant on his excellent taste, Colt concentrated on swallowing his bitter jealousy. It went down worse than his first failed attempt at Bordelaise.

All morning, he'd fluctuated between wallowing in his misery and formulating a plan to win Penny back. But no matter how elaborate each scenario became, it always ended the same way.

He couldn't stay in Poppy Creek, and Penny couldn't leave.

Of course she couldn't. After she'd listed all her reasons, Colt had realized his mistake. He'd lived his whole life on the move, never letting his roots grow deep enough to hold him back. As a result, he'd forgotten how painful it could be if they were suddenly yanked from the ground.

His chest tightening, he sprang from the Adirondack chair and strode a couple paces toward the lake, admiring the reflection of the towering pine trees on the still, sapphire-blue water.

He'd always liked Jack's place. Though only a modest one-bedroom cabin with a small guest house in back, the seclusion a few miles outside of town created a peaceful, restorative atmosphere. When you added the picturesque lake, neighboring forest, and protective mountains in the distance, you had a hidden retreat—a refuge from all of life's problems. Well, *most* of them. No one could hide from heartbreak. At least, not completely.

As he watched a small swallow dive toward the water, breaking the calm surface with its wing tip, he observed the gentle ripple effect. It was strange how one seemingly insignificant decision could have such a far spread influence.

Colt's thoughts drifted to Frank who, at this very moment, was having a much-needed—and healing—heart-to-heart with Beverly. He smiled, recalling the older man's request for him to prepare a pot of tea and a plate of Beverly's favorite scones before he'd left, muttering something about his impending conversation and *if you're going to do it, you might as well do it right.*

For some reason, knowing that Frank—a cantankerous curmudgeon set in his ways—could face his fears and acknowledge his misconceptions had inspired Colt to dig deeper into his own beliefs. Because he couldn't—and wouldn't—give up on Penny. Somehow, he'd find a way to reconcile keeping his promise to his father *and* keeping the woman he loved.

Turning back to face the group, clustered in a half circle by the water's edge under the pretense of lazy Sunday afternoon fishing, Colt did his best to summon the enthusiasm his friend deserved. Announcing his proposal plans should be a happy occasion for Grant. Which was why, when they'd asked Colt about his date with Penny, he'd decided to leave out the last ten minutes of the evening rather than spoil the mood.

"So, what do you guys think of my proposal idea?" Grant returned the ring to its resting place inside the velvet box before slipping it back into his pocket.

His question elicited a far less exuberant response than the ring reveal.

"Come on, guys," Grant cajoled. "It's perfect. You know how much Eliza loves dancing."

"Exactly." Jack leaned forward, repositioning the fishing pole anchored in the ground. "You really want to ruin it by subjecting her to *our* dance moves?"

"Yeah," Reed laughed. "I don't know if you've noticed, but Paul Bunyan over here isn't exactly light on his feet."

"Unless you spend your afternoons pirouetting through the flower beds, I doubt you'll be a backup dancer for Beyoncé anytime soon, either," Jack retorted.

"I'll do most of the heavy lifting where the dancing is concerned," Grant assured them. "You only need to learn a few basic moves."

"I think it's a great idea," Luke offered, recasting his line. "Eliza will love it."

"Thanks, Luke. Sylvia's all set with the costumes."

The mention of costumes sparked more grumbling from Jack and Reed, but Grant ignored them, turning to Colt. "What about you? Can you handle your assignment? The whole proposal hinges on it."

"Uh, yeah. Sure. No problem." Colt shrugged. He'd done it once before.

"Hey! I got one!" Jumping to his feet, Luke jerked back on the pole to set the hook.

Just then, the lilting tune of "The Christmas Waltz" emanated from his back pocket. "That's Cassie," he said with a sheepish grin. Shoving the fishing rod in Colt's hands, he pulled out his phone and stepped away for some privacy.

Colt fumbled with the reel, trying not to lose their only catch of the day. When he'd finally got a firm hold, Luke returned with a somber expression. "Penny needs our help. She can't find Chip."

At his brother's words, Colt released his grip, losing the tension in the line along with the fish.

And his barely restrained emotions.

CHAPTER 26

For the second night in a row, Penny hadn't slept. At some point around 3:00 a.m., she'd abandoned the notion all together. Curled up on the chaise lounge, she kept her eyes glued to the front door in case Chip miraculously decided to come home on his own.

Nearly the entire town had helped her scour every nook and cranny looking for him, but they'd finally paused the search for the night, promising to resume in the morning. And Cassie had insisted she try to get some rest, although the effort had proven to be futile.

A gentle knock stirred Penny from her thoughts, and she immediately scrambled to her feet.

The door eased open, and Cassie poked her head inside, a warm smile illuminating her features. "Guess who's home?"

A joyful sob caught in Penny's throat as Cassie set Chip on the floor.

"You found him!" Falling to her knees, Penny laughed through tears of relief as Chip waddled toward her.

The little stinker didn't appear remotely contrite as he nudged her palm with his head as his form of hello.

"Actually,"—Cassie amended—"Colt did."

Penny's gaze flickered to her friend's face in surprise. "Colt?"

Cassie lowered herself to the carpet, sitting cross-legged. "When most of us went home to sleep, Colt asked Bill Tucker if he could borrow Peggy Sue. Something about pigs being great at finding truffles, so maybe they could track down a tortoise, too." She smiled. "I don't know if Peggy Sue actually proved useful, but they roamed around the nature trail all night until they finally found Chip down by the creek."

Penny's heart raced as she listened to Cassie's story. Colt had searched all night to find him? Tears threatened to spill anew.

Cassie's features softened as she tilted her head, studying her expression. "Colt asked me not to tell you he was the one who found Chip, but I thought you should know." After a pause, she asked gently, "What happened between you two? According to Luke, Colt said you had the perfect date on Saturday. But when I saw him this morning, I'd never seen him look so miserable."

Swallowing against the tightness in her throat, Penny kept her gaze on Chip, nuzzling his head with the tip of her finger. "Things… didn't work out between us."

"Why not?"

All the disappointment and pain from the night beneath the flickering street lamp came rushing back, and Penny blinked rapidly, trying to stave off her burgeoning tears. "Because he's leaving, Cass. For a long time. And I don't think he has plans to come back. Not permanently, anyway."

Cassie remained silent for a long moment, mulling it over. "So, what are you going to do about it?"

Taken aback, Penny straightened. "What do you mean? What *can* I do? I asked him to stay, and he said he can't."

"Did you ask him *why*?"

"No." Penny bit her bottom lip in an attempt to curtail its quivering. "I didn't see the point." She winced at her own lie. "That's not entirely true. I… didn't want to hear his explanation.

Whatever his reason, he'd chosen it over being with me. And I didn't think I could bear it."

Cassie's green eyes filled with compassion, and she offered a small nod in understanding. "Last Christmas, I left Poppy Creek without telling Luke if and when I'd be coming back. At the time, it was an act of hopelessness."

Penny waited in patient silence for her to continue, recalling bits and pieces of what had transpired between them.

"Well, as you know…" She trailed off, a dreamy, contented smile curling the edges of her mouth. "Luke came after me. And weeks later, when I asked him what went through his mind in that moment, you know what he said?"

Penny gave a slight shake of her head.

"Luke said he knew there were things outside his control, but he also knew if he didn't try everything in his power to fight for me, he'd regret it for the rest of his life. And if he'd learned anything from losing his father, it was that he didn't want to leave this earth with regrets."

As Cassie's words seeped through the cracks in her walls, Penny wasn't quite sure how to process them.

Cassie leaned forward, her gaze earnest. "If you were to die today, what would you regret not doing?"

To Penny's surprise, the vision of a faded white envelope flashed before her eyes.

*

*E*ven before Colt reached Luke's workshop, he smelled the invigorating aroma of sawdust and varnish.

And when he stepped through the sliding barn door, he was immediately struck by the breadth of the space. Lumber in every width, length, and wood grain imaginable, shelves bursting with an assortment of fasteners and fixtures, and more power tools than Colt even knew existed—all neatly organized. Not to mention the array of expertly crafted furniture in various stages of completion.

At the crunch of wood scraps beneath his feet, Colt drew his brother's attention from his current project.

"Hey." Luke acknowledged him with a quick glance before giving the strange object one last swipe with the square of sandpaper. At Colt's frown of confusion, Luke explained, "It's a quilt rack for Frida Connelly. Apparently, she's outgrown the three others I've already made her."

"Her place must look like a quilt museum by now." Colt flashed a lopsided grin, too tired to form a full-on smile.

"You look terrible," Luke pointed out, setting down the swatch of sandpaper. "I suppose it has something to do with your heroic, middle-of-the-night rescue of one wayfaring tortoise. And perhaps whatever happened with said tortoise's owner." Striding to a mini fridge in the corner, he cracked open the small door, revealing an assortment of glistening bottles. He removed a cream soda and a sarsaparilla, handing the latter to Colt.

"Thanks." Colt popped off the cap on the edge of Luke's drafting table.

"Want to talk about it?" His brother used the same method to open his bottle, just like their father taught them, much to their mother's dismay.

"Well, I'm not here to build a birdhouse," Colt said ruefully.

Chuckling, Luke nodded toward his workbench, while he perched on a backless barstool.

Once settled on the bench, Colt leaned forward, both forearms poised on his thighs while he stared at the sawdust-covered floor. "How'd you do it?" he finally asked, barely loud enough for Luke to hear him.

"Do what?"

"Quit Dad's practice when you knew how much it meant to him that you'd taken it over?" His tone held no censure, only urgent curiosity.

"It wasn't easy," Luke admitted after a long, thoughtful pause. "Ultimately, it was something Mom said that helped me make the decision."

Colt glanced up, watching his brother closely. "What did she say?"

Luke twisted the bottle in his hand, the dark, amber-colored glass glinting in the sunlight streaming through the open door. He took a sip before slowly lowering it, as if collecting his thoughts. "She said Dad would be proud of me. Not because I'd taken over his practice, but because of the man I'd become." His voice thickened with emotion, and he roughly cleared his throat. "She said as parents, they try to pass on what they know, but at some point, you have to lean into the person God created you to be, and their wisdom becomes a guide more than an ultimatum." Luke paused, studying him intently. "Why do you ask?"

His palm moist from condensation on the bottle—and perhaps nerves—Colt wiped his hand on his shorts. "Dad made me promise him something before he died. And I'm having a hard time keeping it. Truthfully, I don't know if I *want* to keep it anymore."

Silence filled the space between them, save for twittering birds in the distance.

They'd never discussed how Colt was the last one to see their father alive. Or how he'd been the one to watch him die.

"What was it?" Luke asked gently.

Colt squeezed his eyes shut as the vision of his father's frail body lying in the hospital bed forced its way to the forefront of his mind. He could still hear the beeping of the heart monitor and smell the overpowering aroma of cleaning supplies mingled with the white peonies his mother kept in a vase by the window.

His father had just finished lamenting their unused plane tickets, and how he'd promised their mother a trip around the world. She wanted to dance on the beach beneath the moonlight and taste exotic foods she couldn't find in Poppy Creek.

With trembling fingers, his father had reached for his hand. At the memory, Colt gulped against the emotion lodged in his throat. No matter how hard he tried, he couldn't forget the sensation of his father's cold, limp grasp or how his once large, meaty hands had turned to papery skin and bones.

Wrenching his eyes open, Colt met his brother's gaze. "He made me promise not to waste a single second of my life, but to live each moment as if it were my last. Dad regretted not taking Mom on that trip, missing out on all the experiences they'd dreamt about all those years. I think he didn't want me to get stuck here, always saying one day I'd live my life, but never actually doing it."

Realization lit Luke's hazel eyes. "That's why you're always traveling, pushing the limits, and never settling down."

"I never minded before," Colt disclosed with complete sincerity. "I viewed my promise to Dad as a gift, for him and myself. The adventures I've had... they've all been incredible. I've done things most only dream of. But..." He trailed off, a brief glimpse of Penny's radiant smile derailing his thoughts.

All at once, he missed her so much, his chest hurt. He set the bottle of sarsaparilla on the workbench, unable to drink another drop.

"Colt," Luke said slowly. "Did you ever think Dad's thoughts may not be as interconnected as you assumed?"

"What do you mean?"

"I mean, *Dad* regretted not having those experiences with Mom. But telling *you* not to waste your life doesn't necessarily mean the same thing."

"I don't understand what you're trying to say." Colt's voice rose a little in frustration.

Luke set his bottle on the drafting table and leaned forward, his brows lowered in careful consideration of his next words. "Maybe Dad wasn't expecting you to live a high-octane life. Maybe he simply meant don't miss out on the things that matter to you. For Dad, it was not taking Mom on that trip. But for you, it could be something else. Or maybe some*one* else."

As his brother spoke, a tremendous weight lifted from Colt's shoulders. And for the second time in forty-eight hours, unshed tears pooled in his eyes.

All these years, he'd operated under a solitary—and faulty—assumption.

But in hindsight, he wouldn't necessarily do anything differently. He appreciated his wealth of experiences.

But looking forward…

His new perspective could change everything.

CHAPTER 27

*a*s Penny clutched the smooth, white envelope in her hand, it felt almost hot to the touch, as if the words inside were burning to get out.

The long-awaited moment left her breathless, poised on the edge of a proverbial precipice—once she jumped, she couldn't turn back.

But Cassie's wisdom resonated with a simple truth—time on this earth wasn't a guarantee. And the mere thought of never reading her father's letter made her heart break.

In preparation, she'd drawn the curtains in his office for the first time since he'd passed away. Sunlight filtered through the filmy glass, highlighting specks of dust dancing in the air.

Penny smiled, recalling how her father once told her the tiny particles were microscopic fairies. She'd pranced around the apartment trying to capture them in a glass jar, giggling as they darted out of reach. Of course, she never did catch one. But looking back, she realized that was never really the point.

Seated at his desk, she withdrew a silver letter opener. Her fingers trembled as she inserted the sharp tip in the top right corner. Inhaling a deep breath, she tried to steady her hand. With a quick flick of her wrist, she broke the seal, the gentle tear echoing in her eardrums.

Suddenly overcome with emotion, she placed the envelope and opener on the desk, and sprang from her seat with anxious energy. Wringing her hands, she paced the threadbare carpet, gazing up at the ceiling as she fought back tears.

In the next few minutes, she had so much to lose and everything to gain.

Wrestling with her tumultuous thoughts, she exhaled slowly before sitting back down.

Gingerly, she removed a single sheet of paper from its resting place. As she unfolded it, ironing out the creases against the flat surface of the tabletop, silent tears dampened the page.

Her father's handwriting greeted her like a welcome-home hug after a long absence—its emotional resonance bittersweet.

As she read, she kept one hand on the letter, one hand clasped over her mouth to restrain a rising sob.

The letter was dated the day before he died.

Sweet P,

I want to start by telling you how incredibly proud I am of the woman you've become. Not only are you gracious and kind, beautiful inside and out, but you're braver than I ever imagined. Especially after everything I taught you to fear. I can only assume that despite my shortcomings, a bit of your mother's adventurous light sparked somewhere deep inside of you. And for that, I'm eternally grateful.

Never lose that light, Sweet P. Just be careful you don't let it burn out of control or it will consume you like a wildfire, destroying everything in its path. Much like it did to your mother.

I'm writing this letter as a confession, of sorts. A means of accountability to do the right thing, despite my trepidation regarding the outcome. Whatever happens, you deserve to know the truth behind my efforts.

After all these years, I've never stopped loving your mother or pursuing her. And just before your fourth birthday, I learned she'd been living in a women's shelter in Starcross Cove, just a few hours away.

The words blurred on the page as Penny choked back a sob, tears searing her eyes. *The women's shelter... the beach where she'd built a sandcastle with Colt...* Her temples throbbed as she struggled to make sense of the jumbled pieces.

Forcing the air in and out of her lungs with ragged breaths, she concentrated on the rest of the letter.

As much as it breaks my heart to admit this to you, your mother's thirst for adventure led her down a dark path of substance abuse and dangerous choices. But she'd finally sought help. Hearing the news gave me extraordinary hope. And like two brave knights on a quest, you and I left Poppy Creek to bring her back home.

As you can guess, our expedition didn't go quite as I'd planned. When we arrived, I learned she'd had another child with someone else, less than a year after she'd left us. And she had no interest in rejoining our family.

Penny's chest rose and fell with each racking sob as she realized the two girls in the photograph weren't merely strangers bound to her by childhood daydreams, so lifelike they felt like a memory. All this time, her father had kept a secret hidden in plain sight. And she wasn't sure how she'd ever forgive him for that.

At the time, you were too young to remember or grasp the significance of that day. And I chose to keep it a secret with the belief I was protecting you from insurmountable pain. But now as you're away at college, braving the world on your own, I realize what an untenable mistake I made. Lacking my own courage, I'd underestimated your strength.

Watching you spread your wings has been the most beautiful sight a father could ever behold. And I'm reminded of what our favorite poet, Robert Frost, once said....

"There is freedom in being bold."

You, Sweet P, are not your mother or your father.

Your wings are guided by both passion and prudence. And I trust you to fly with a sense of adventure and sound judgment.

Oh, the heights you will reach because you have respect for the ground.

Today, I go on a solo quest. I learned your mother has returned to the women's shelter and I plan to try one last time. But whether I return alone or not, you will receive this letter, my sincerest apology, and my faithful promise to answer any other questions you might have.

All my love,

Dad

Hunched over the desk, Penny buried her face in her hands, her shoulders shaking uncontrollably as each sob tore through her body. The cruel irony of her father's letter—and the fact that he'd never come home at all—proved too much for her weary heart to withstand.

He'd called her brave, and yet, he'd never know that the day she received the phone call about his death, she'd returned home and closed herself off from the outside world.

She wasn't bold. And she certainly wasn't free.

Fear crippled her, to the point she couldn't even confront Colt about his decision to leave Poppy Creek. Or more importantly, to leave her behind.

Her thoughts drifted to the photograph of the two girls building a sandcastle. Somewhere out there she had a sister. Penny found the thought impossible to comprehend.

So much in her life was about to change. And she had a choice....

Did she cower in fear?

Or embrace it with courage?

*H*is heart hammering in his chest, Colt brought the spoon to his lips. A lot was riding on this concoction, and it needed to be perfect.

Taking a slow sip, his eyes brightened in excitement. *Bingo!* After three failed attempts, the coffee marinade tasted like pure, caffeinated heaven. After making a quick notation on the recipe card, Colt pulled the steaks out of the refrigerator.

Since he planned to wow Jack at the Fourth of July cook-off in two days, and the steaks needed that long to marinate, he wouldn't have time for a complete dry run. He'd have to cross his fingers and hope for the best.

A deafening blare shook through the house, and Colt nearly dropped the steaks on the kitchen floor. Recovering from the shock, he slid them on the counter before wiping his hands on a dish towel, shaking his head ruefully.

Making his way into Frank's study, Colt shot a stern frown at the rabble-rouser lounging in the chenille recliner. "I'm really regretting not going with Beverly's suggestion of a soft, tinkling bell."

With a wry grin, Frank brandished the bullhorn. "But this is much more effective, don't you think?"

"If your main objective is ruining both of our hearing."

As Frank chuckled, Colt marveled at the huge shift in his mood ever since he'd had a heart-to-heart with Beverly.

"What can I get for you, Your Highness?" Colt bent forward in an exaggerated bow, complete with a hand flourish.

"I need a favor. But first,"—Frank sniffed the air—"are you developing a top secret war tactic for the government? I've been smelling coffee all afternoon but haven't seen a single drop."

Colt snorted in laughter. "Sorry. I *have* been working on a top secret project. But I promise, I wasn't trying to torture you. I'll grab you a cup."

Popping back into the kitchen, Colt filled a lightweight ceramic mug with the brewed coffee left over from the marinade.

Returning to the study, he handed it to Frank. "So, what's this favor?"

For a moment, Colt thought he noticed the old man's cheeks tinge pink. But it could've been from the steam curling above the brim of the mug.

Frank took a languid sip, showing marked improvement in using his left hand since his fall. Setting the mug on the TV stand situated near the recliner, he nodded toward his desk. "Bring me the laptop."

Dutifully, Colt brought the laptop along with a bamboo tray to rest it on. As he flipped it open in front of Frank, the screen flickered to life.

Startled by the image on display, Colt darted his gaze to the old man's face. No doubt about it—his weathered cheeks were decidedly rosy.

Frank cleared his throat. "I need you to pick this up for me."

Glancing back at the listing, Colt noticed the antiques store was located in San Francisco. The errand would take most of the day. But for something this important? It was definitely worth it.

"It will be my pleasure."

"Thank you," Frank grunted, visibly uncomfortable.

As Colt returned the laptop to the desk and wrote down the pertinent information, he couldn't help a smile.

Apparently, he wasn't the only one who had big plans for the future.

CHAPTER 28

*S*ince reading her father's letter, Penny found it difficult to go about her daily tasks as if nothing happened, when everything had changed in an instant.

And the longer she spent cataloging and pricing new antiques, the more the niggling idea in the back of her mind solidified into a fully-fledged plan.

Entering the store from the storage room, Penny discovered Bree draping a vintage evening gown over a decorative dress form. The girl sighed dreamily as the blush-colored silk folds fell to the ground, pooling in a graceful puddle. "Don't you love fashion from the 1930s? I think it's becoming my favorite era. In fact, I find myself having less of a desire to wear anything else."

"It suits you." Penny smiled. With her flirty, calf-length skirt and bolero jacket, Bree could fit right in with the glamorous company of Greta Garbo and Joan Crawford. "Do you mind holding down the fort while I pop over to Maggie's for a few minutes?"

"Sure. I'm almost done with the dresses, but there's a stack of hat boxes with my name on it." Bree displayed a gleeful grin. "I'm hoping to find a beret just like the one Marlene Dietrich always wore."

Suddenly moved with affection for her sweet, spirited employee, Penny sighed. "What am I going to do without you?"

"Well," Bree glanced at the floor, twisting the sole of her black-and-white Oxford into the scuffed hardwood. "I've been meaning to talk to you about that…."

Bree hesitated, and Penny recalled the strained conversation they'd had in the storage room several days earlier. The one where she now realized she'd given atrocious advice.

"I've… decided not to go to college after all." Her gaze flickered to Penny's face, sadness evident in the dull sheen of her usually vibrant eyes. "Would you consider hiring me full-time?"

The enormity of Bree's question weighed heavily on Penny's shoulders, and she hated to see the resignation written across the girl's face. "Bree," she said softly. "You know I'd love nothing more than to keep you forever. But…"

At the small, yet worrisome word, Bree winced.

Drawing in a fortifying breath, Penny continued. "But first, I need you to tell me why you've decided not to go to college."

Defensive, Bree stiffened. "Like I told you, I don't want to be homesick. I'd miss my family and friends too much."

"Is that all?" she asked gently, suspecting her fears ran much deeper than that.

Bree's face fell, her shoulders slumped in heartbreaking dejection.

Taking her hand, Penny led her toward a vintage chaise lounge—the same style as the one in her apartment, but upholstered in a vivid plum-colored velvet. Pulling Bree down beside her, Penny kept a grip on her hand. "A few days ago, you said something about being afraid to be different. What did you mean by that?"

Although she had her own suspicions, she wanted the girl to

express the thought out loud and relinquish some of its power over her.

Her face twisting with suppressed tears, Bree gestured toward her outfit with an agitated flick of her wrist. "Isn't it obvious? I'm a freak show."

Penny cringed at the harsh term, insisting, "You are not."

"Yes, I am!" Bree cried hoarsely. "And the worst part is, I've tried not to be. I even bought a pair of jeans and a T-shirt. But when I looked in the mirror"—she paused, brushing a wayward tear from her eye—"I didn't look like *me* anymore. How pathetic is that?"

"It's not pathetic at all." Penny squeezed her hand. "And if you want your entire wardrobe to consist of outfits from the 1930s, you go right ahead."

"But they'll make fun of me," Bree whimpered.

"Maybe," Penny answered honestly. "But if they have any sense, they'll realize that decade held more glamour in a single suede glove than our generation can claim in an entire high-end fashion line."

"That's true," Bree grinned through her tears.

"If you're really worried about it,"—Penny added—"you can try pairing some pieces from that era with more modern clothing. But in the end, you can't live your life afraid of other people's opinions. What's in here,"—she said, tapping her heart—"is much more important than the outside embellishments. And you, my dear, are the sweetest, smartest, most hardworking and caring woman I know. And I promise you, the people of Santa Barbara will come to see that, too. No matter what you're wearing."

Before Penny had finished her speech, Bree threw her arms around her neck, hugging her tightly. "Will you come visit me?"

"Try to stop me," Penny promised.

And to her surprise, the words spilled from her lips without a moment's hesitation.

*S*tanding on a bustling street corner in San Francisco left a strange emptiness in the pit of Colt's stomach. And with each step he took toward the unremarkable antiques shop, he felt Penny's absence more acutely.

Normally, he'd relish the opportunity for a change in scenery. But being away from the woman he loved seemed to drain most of the enjoyment from the day's excursion. His thoughts perpetually drifted to what she might be doing in that moment and whether she was thinking of him, too.

Pushing through the front door, he nearly stumbled backward in surprise. He'd expected the establishment to at least hold a passing resemblance to Thistle & Thorn, yet the dull, uninspired space couldn't be more different. The grid-like shelving units possessed none of the whimsy or magic, although many of the items themselves were similar.

Colt's chest swelled with pride, realizing Thistle & Thorn was a reflection of its owner. And Penny's passion and vibrant imagination was something no other shop owner could replicate, even if they wanted to. The store, like its owner, was truly one of a kind.

"Can I help you?" The tired, uninterested clerk barely tore his gaze from the flat-screen TV displaying some low-budget action movie Colt had never seen before.

"I'm looking for this." He held out a slip of paper with an item number printed in bold letters. "I called earlier to place it on hold."

With an irritated sigh, the man snatched the paper from Colt's hand. "I'll be right back." Clearly put out, he ducked into the back room, casting one last glance over his shoulder at the TV before disappearing from view.

As Colt waited, he held his breath, nauseated by the unpleasant combination of cigarette smoke and an overly sweet and artificial-smelling air freshener. Penny's shop, on the other hand, smelled like dried lavender, old books, and unexplored treasures. If he could, he'd wrap himself in the aroma like a comforting blanket.

Recognizing his thoughts had reached romance novel-level cheesiness, he laughed out loud. But his amusement was cut short by the shrill ring of his cell phone. His mind still lingering on Penny, Colt answered without checking the caller ID.

"Finally! I've been trying to get a hold of you for days." His friend's irritation echoed through the speakers.

"Sorry, Bryce. I've been meaning to call. But I needed some time to think over your offer."

"What's there to think about? You've been begging me for this job for years."

Colt winced, guilt weighing on his heart. The new scuba diving operation *had* been his idea. Which would make his next words all the more difficult. "I know, and I'm really sorry to do this, but—"

Bryce groaned so loud Colt yanked the phone away from his ear.

"What happened? Don't tell me your girl vetoed the idea. The Colt I know wouldn't let a woman stand in the way of such a great opportunity."

"That's the thing, Bryce. She's not standing in the way."

His friend snorted in disbelief.

"I'm serious. It's not like that. She simply… presented a more appealing opportunity."

Silence filled the speaker for a long moment before Bryce answered, "She must be pretty special, then."

"She is," Colt said with conviction.

"Fine," Bryce sighed. "Then, I'll try to be happy for you. But if you change your mind, let me know."

"I will." But even as Colt said goodbye, he knew that would never happen.

As soon as he'd made the decision to stay in Poppy Creek, he hadn't regretted it for a second.

And once he finalized the details of his grand plan, he'd lay his heart on the line, praying Penny would give him another chance.

When the disgruntled clerk returned with Frank's item, Colt hoped with fervent optimism that one day soon he'd be picking up an engagement ring of his own.

And he couldn't wait.

CHAPTER 29

Strumming his fingertips against the kitchen counter, Colt watched the dark, chocolatey liquid drip slowly through the paper filter into the glass carafe. Based on the aromatic steam wafting toward him, he'd done something right.

Colt knew he'd taken a big risk sneaking out to the roasting barn at the crack of dawn without Frank. He also knew his special blend could turn out to be a total flop.

But if it wasn't, it could be the key to earning Frank's respect... and so much more.

He glanced at the vintage avocado-green wall clock—7:05 a.m.

Frank should be awake by now.

After setting the carafe and two mugs—one for himself and one for Frank—on a serving tray, Colt carried it down the hallway toward Frank's room, detouring when he heard voices echoing from the den.

He hesitated in the doorway, surprised to find Cassie poised on the edge of the couch, holding up a sketchpad for Frank, who lounged in the recliner.

Hearing him enter, Cassie glanced up and smiled. "Good morning."

"Uh, good morning." His gaze darted between them. The mornings were the busiest time of day for the café, so Cassie didn't usually arrive to work on their manuscript until later in the afternoon.

Before he could ask the reason for her visit, Cassie tilted her head back, sniffing the air. "Whatever that is, it smells heavenly. And there's a hint of something I can't quite place."

The corner of Colt's mouth quirked up slightly. His sister-in-law had a reputation for an impeccable palate and sense of smell. He would take great pride in finally stumping her. "I took the liberty of creating a new blend." He stole a sideways glance at Frank as he slid the tray onto the coffee table.

Frank didn't bat an eye, his expression unreadable.

"I'm intrigued. May I?" She reached for the carafe, and Colt nodded, his pulse racing as she poured herself a cup.

Slow and deliberate, Cassie brought the mug to her lips, inhaling deeply before taking her first sip. She swirled the concoction in her mouth a moment, letting it coat every taste bud before swallowing. Her eyes instantly sparked with delight. "Colt, this is delicious! It's bright and floral with—" She took another sip, her smile lines deepening. "Is that a hint of honey I'm tasting?"

"That's from the Guatemalan beans," Colt told her, encouraged by her reaction. "I blended them with a wet process Ethiopian bean. I took them to four hundred and ten degrees. Darker than a blonde roast, but light enough to maintain that crisp, citrusy finish."

"Well, I'm impressed." Setting down her mug, she filled the second one. "Frank, you need to try this."

His hands suddenly clammy, Colt wiped them on his jeans before grabbing the mug Cassie offered him. After passing it to Frank, he took a step back, his heart thrumming wildly as he studied each infinitesimal twitch of an eyebrow or flare of a nostril.

For what felt like hours, Frank didn't take a sip at all. He merely swished the hot liquid in languid, methodical motions, staring intently into the black, velvety depths.

Unable to bear the agonizing silence, Colt blurted, "Sir, I realize I may have stepped out of line creating this blend on my own. But I'd hoped you'd appreciate my initiative. And if it turns out to be halfway decent, I—" He sucked in a breath, blood pumping inside his eardrums. "I would be honored and grateful if, even after you've returned to work, you'd consider hiring me as a secondary roaster. Of course, I realize there's only enough work for part-time hours, but I'd love to help fulfill the growing café and online orders, plus the various nonprofits you supply."

Winded by his impromptu monologue, Colt inhaled sharply, trying to regain his equilibrium. A huge part of his future now hung in the balance. And the outcome seemed fuzzy and uncertain at best.

The truth was, due to the side effects from Frank's heart medication, his sense of taste fluctuated on a regular basis. And if Colt had inexplicably chosen an off day...

He cringed, pushing the thought aside.

Forgoing a reply, Frank took a leisurely sip, slurping as he did so. While not the politest gesture under normal circumstances, Colt knew from *The Mariposa Method* that slurping aerated the coffee, spreading it across the tongue and palate, engaging the full spectrum of sensations.

As Frank swallowed, all the air in the room seemed to evaporate, and even the soothing tick of the grandfather clock faded into the background.

Colt leaned forward, straining to hear Frank's unspoken words.

"Well, what do you think?" Cassie asked, putting Colt out of his misery.

"I'd take the temperature ten degrees higher next time, but it's not bad."

"Next time?" Colt repeated, his tone tentative. "Does that mean...?"

"I could use some extra hands around here," Frank admitted. "Especially if there's a honeymoon on the horizon..." As he trailed off, a faint blush crept across his cheeks.

"Woo-hoo! Thank you!" Colt pumped his fist in the air, while Cassie cheered from her perch on the couch.

Colt expected Frank to squirm in discomfort and insist they settle down. But instead, an uncharacteristically broad smile stretched across his face.

"This calls for some pastries with our coffee, don't you think?" Frank asked, taking another sip.

"That's a wonderful idea!" Cassie beamed. "I think there are some scones in the kitchen." She stood and turned to Colt. "Why don't I grab another mug so you can join us? We're going over Frank's proposal plans for tonight, since they'll have guaranteed privacy while we're all at the Fourth of July Festival."

"Sounds great. But I have something even better than scones. I'll be right back."

Practically skipping down the hallway in his elation, Colt halted in front of his makeshift bedroom. He'd bought another box of baklava while in San Francisco yesterday, and it would make the perfect celebratory treat.

As he nudged open the creaking door, he froze in surprise.

The barrage of cardboard boxes littering the floor had disappeared. And his twin mattress now rested on a simple wrought iron frame. The ironing board and other miscellaneous items... all gone.

His gaze traveled the newly uncluttered space, coming to rest on a sleek mahogany dresser. He immediately recognized his brother's handiwork.

Inching closer, Colt plucked a notecard from the smooth surface and scanned the message in disbelief.

Proud of you.

Three simple words. And yet, they filled a gaping hole in his heart he'd been ignoring for years.

Still stunned, Colt took in the surreal surroundings once more. Somehow, in the two hours he'd been out in the barn roasting, Luke and Cassie—and perhaps others—had transformed the storage space into an actual bedroom.

He cracked a smile. The whole time he'd had his secret plan up his sleeve, they'd pulled off an even bigger one. And while he'd been intent on proving himself to Frank, the old man had already given his seal of approval.

His chest tight with emotion, Colt ran a hand along the polished woodgrain, more assured than ever in his decision to stay in Poppy Creek.

After a lifetime of wandering, he finally had a home.

⭐

*E*merging from Thistle & Thorn onto the bustling sidewalk of Main Street, Penny nearly ran right into the broad chest of Bill Tucker.

"Whoopsie daisy! Sorry, Penny," the giant farmer drawled. "Peggy Sue's in a rush for some corn on the cob."

Sure enough, the rotund pig tugged on her leash, her curly tail nearly straight from the exertion.

"No problem." Penny watched with a bemused smile as Peggy Sue's pink, waddling rump disappeared into the crowd.

All four streets surrounding the town square swarmed with activity. Patriotic bunting draped from the rooftops and red-white-and-blue streamers swirled around every lamppost.

The warm, golden gleam of the late afternoon sun lent the scene a nostalgic, dreamy glow, as though the moment were a snapshot of an idyllic memory.

Penny scanned the white billowy tents dotting the cobbled streets, searching for Mac Houston's iconic booth. Every Fourth of July, he hosted a fundraiser called the Sizzle & Surprise, which also happened to be the fifth and final activity on the list for the guidebook.

To participate in the culinary adventure, each entrant bought a raffle ticket. This year, the proceeds went toward the animal shelter in Primrose Valley. The ticket provided entry into the mystery food competition. The "sizzle" derived from each food being deep-fried in hot oil. But the "surprise" element was the thrilling part.

The participants had to guess the base of each battered morsel —half a dozen in total. The person who got all six correct won a week's worth of free groceries from Mac's Mercantile.

The foods changed annually, but always ranged from unusual, like deep-fried Jell-O, to downright unpalatable, like deep-fried caterpillar. Sometimes Mac left clues. Penny suspected the sixth item in the lineup belonged to the pepper family, considering a suspicious-looking stem protruded from the ball of fried dough. She'd have to make sure Colt steered clear of that one.

At the thought of Colt, her stomach fluttered. She had so much to tell him, starting with the arrangement she'd made with his mother yesterday. In doing so, she'd taken a huge risk, and she prayed he would appreciate the gesture.

Her breath stalled in her throat when she caught sight of him heading toward her. He looked so calm and carefree striding through the swell of townsfolk and tourists in his American flag board shorts and white tee. In fact, he appeared to be in *too* good of a mood, all things considered. Almost as if their breakup hadn't crushed his heart into a thousand tiny pieces as it had hers.

Apprehension pulsed through her veins, leaving her light-headed. Had she made a mistake talking to Maggie? Maybe she should cut her losses and move on. Clearly, Colt had.

Sucking in a breath, she squared her shoulders, unwilling to let her fears and negative thoughts overwhelm her. She'd come too far to give into them now. Regardless of the outcome, she wouldn't be left wondering *what if.*

"Hi." Colt stood two feet in front of her, his turquoise-blue eyes shining with... what? Excitement? Exhilaration? Hope? She wasn't sure. But she found the way his intense gaze bored into hers unnerving, to say the least.

"Hi," she answered, her voice wobbly.

"I have our raffle tickets, but first—"

"I have something to say," they blurted in unison.

"Sorry." Penny's cheeks flushed. Could she be more of a bumbling mess?

"Mind if I go first?" Colt ran his fingers through his hair, a mannerism Penny had come to recognize.

Was it possible he was just as nervous?

"Sure." She cast a self-conscious glance at Mac, who sat in a camping chair inside the booth, observing them with open curiosity. Her cheeks heated hotter than his frying oil, but she turned her attention back on Colt, choosing to ignore their captive audience.

Colt met her gaze with an earnest tenderness that made everyone around them disappear, and her heartbeat stilled when he reached for her hand. "I have a confession. All the crazy adventures I've had, it's what I thought my dad wanted for me. And I never questioned it... until you." His gaze fell to their entwined fingers and Penny shivered, either from his words or the way his thumb caressed her skin. He locked eyes with her once more, this time with a stirring soulfulness that stole her breath."The world has never looked more beautiful to me than when I see it through your eyes. And the only adventure I want is a life with you."

Weakened by his heartfelt admission, Penny struggled to find her voice. "Wh-what exactly are you saying?"

"I'm saying… I'm not going anywhere. I'm all in. With you. This town. And all the little things that make this place our home." He glanced at the row of chafing dishes. "Starting right here, with the final item on our list, but the first of many more adventures to come." Plucking the fried glob by the stem, he brought it toward his lips. And before Penny could stop him, he popped the entire thing in his mouth.

She watched, in horror, as he chewed, his eyes bulging in shock. His entire face contorted, his cheeks flaming bright red as tears streamed down his cheeks.

Mac sprang from his seat. "Is he okay? I knew ghost peppers were hot, but he looks like he might pass out."

"I'm fine," Colt croaked hoarsely, in visible pain. When he finally swallowed the offending pepper, he whimpered, "Although, a glass of milk would be nice."

On impulse, Penny popped onto her tiptoes and kissed him deeply, releasing a short gasp as the pungent spice hit her lips. After a long, languorous moment, she pulled away, murmuring, "Did that help?"

"Much better," he moaned softly. "One more time should do the trick."

With a breathy laugh, she eagerly obliged.

CHAPTER 30

*T*he sweetness of Penny's kiss mingled with the fiery spice of the pepper, alleviating some of the burn. Although, Colt had to admit, the tingling heat heightened the sensation of her lips against his, and he wouldn't mind exploring the phenomenon a bit more.

"I think my mouth is numb," Penny breathed when their lips finally parted.

"I'll take that as a compliment." He flashed a devilish grin, and she laughed, shooting a rippling warmth through his entire body.

Oh, how he'd missed that sound.

As her laughter subsided, she gazed up at him, her coppery eyes filled with wonder. "I still can't believe you're staying."

"You don't mind, do you?" he teased.

"No," she said slowly, her lips twisting in a smile. "But it does present a small problem."

"What do you mean?" His heartbeat faltered.

"I don't know what I'm going to do with my ticket to Greece." She lifted her shoulders in a tiny shrug, and Colt's mouth fell open.

"Your what?"

"Your mom and I were planning to come visit you." A pretty blush swept across her cheeks as she gazed up at him through thick lashes. "But I suppose, now that you're not going... if you want to come *with* us..."

She trailed off, and Colt feared his heart might burst from happiness. He couldn't believe she'd bought a plane ticket. And the fact that she'd thought to include his mother only made him love her more. "A trip to Greece with my two favorite women? I can't imagine anything better." In his excitement, he plucked her from the ground, spun in a half circle, and let her slowly slip down the length of his arms until their lips met once more.

He'd never experienced a bigger rush than Penny's kiss; each one left him simultaneously satiated and hungry for more.

A throat cleared behind him, and Colt reluctantly glanced over his shoulder.

"I hate to interrupt, Romeo,"—Jack said with an enormous grin—"but we're up." Turning to Penny, he added, "I don't know if you're aware, but your boyfriend has entered the barbecue cook-off this year."

Penny flushed at Jack's use of the term *boyfriend*, but to Colt's delight, she appeared pleased with the moniker.

"You did?" she asked him, with a touch of surprise.

"Yep." He slid his arm around her waist, drawing her closer. "And I plan to win, too."

Jack snorted in amusement. "You realize I haven't lost in over a decade, right?"

"So you're saying a new champion is overdue?" Colt raised his eyebrows in a challenging smirk.

"Ha! Touché, Davis." Jack slapped him on the shoulder. "Shall we make things interesting and place a wager?"

"I was hoping you'd say that." Colt's mouth went dry in anticipation of his next words.

Jack narrowed his gaze in interest. "What do you have in mind?"

"Well..." Colt subtly tightened his grip on Penny's waist, gathering courage. "If you win, I'll bus tables at the diner for a month, free of charge."

"I like the sound of that!"

"But if *I* win," Colt continued, his pulse quickening. "You'll hire me as a part-time chef."

Jack blinked, momentarily taken aback. But as he glanced from Colt to Penny, then back at Colt, his rugged features softened. "You're serious, aren't you?"

"More than almost anything else in my life." Before Jack could beat him to the joke, he added, "Which I realize isn't saying a lot, but—"

"Say no more." Jack held up his hand. "If you want a job, you've got one. Win or lose."

"Really?" Colt's pulse sputtered as he fluctuated between amazement and overwhelming gratitude.

"With a few conditions."

"Such as?"

"For starters, you'll be *sous*-chef, second-in-command to yours truly."

"Fair enough," Colt chuckled. "And?"

Jack's cornflower-blue eyes twinkled mischievously. "*And...* you have to learn all the diner lingo."

Colt released a good-natured groan. "You run a hard bargain, my friend. But you've got yourself a deal."

As they shook hands, Colt kept one arm around Penny, savoring the quiet whisper of contentment that stole over him.

Thrills and adventures may look different going forward, but Colt could say with unwavering certainty that his life had never been fuller.

And he knew, in his heart of hearts, that he'd fulfilled his promise *and* made his father proud.

⭐

*a*s the sun dipped behind the tall steeple of the courthouse, Penny's throat tightened with emotion. She couldn't recall a single moment in time when she'd felt more at peace.

Huddled among her group of lifelong friends, she laughed as Colt and Jack stood on a cramped, makeshift stage, both clutching the blue first-place ribbon commemorating their tie. Though she loved the two men dearly, *sharing* wasn't their strong suit. She could only imagine the antics they'd get into trying to work together.

They hopped off the platform, disappearing from sight as they were swallowed by the crowd gathered in the street.

Mayor Burns took the stage dressed in a slick gray suit, which had to be sweltering on a hot July evening. But the man had a habit of prioritizing appearance over comfort.

As he recited a lengthy and grandiose speech, Penny scanned for signs of Colt, but she couldn't catch a glimpse of him anywhere. "Where do you think Colt and Jack went?"

"I don't know, but I don't see Grant, either." Eliza bounced on the balls of her feet, trying to peek over the wall of shoulders.

"Luke and Reed are missing, too." Cassie frowned.

Penny took a few steps backward onto the lawn, trying to get a vantage point away from the throng of people packed on the street and sidewalk.

Tick, tick, tick...

The unexpected ticking sound preceded an ominous hiss. Glancing down, she gasped in horror as shiny black sprinkler heads sprang from the ground.

Oh, no... not again! Colt wouldn't... would he?

Before she had time to answer her own question, Penny shrieked as a blast of water spewed from every direction. She leapt to safety, nearly tackling Cassie and Eliza in her haste.

Startled cries filled the air as everyone scrambled farther away from the lawn.

"Colt!" Mayor Burns bellowed, his face bright red.

Penny's heart sank. How could Colt do something so irresponsible... *twice?*

Amid the pandemonium, a loudspeaker crackled.

The clamoring slowly died down as Gene Kelly's iconic voice resonated crisp and clear above the town square.

"Doodle-loo-doo-doo-doodle-loo-doo..."

At the same time, all five missing men emerged from The Calendar Café wearing yellow raincoats and felt fedoras while brandishing long black umbrellas.

Eliza squealed, jumping up and down in exuberant excitement as they sauntered into the center of the lawn, performing a jaunty, truncated version of "Singin' in the Rain" with Grant as the focal point.

Penny gaped in complete astonishment, along with everyone else in town, as they strutted their stuff through the thematic spray of water.

Before long, the crowd started to sing along, clapping and cheering as it became apparent the impromptu performance held far more significance than a silly prank.

Penny's eyes welled with tears as she watched the men put their pride aside to make Eliza's dream proposal come true. While some might consider choreographing a dance to a favorite musical a bit over-the-top, the expression on Eliza's face showcased just how much it meant to her. And Penny couldn't have been more overjoyed for her friend.

As the guys lined up, one in front of the other for the grand finale, Penny noticed Colt sneak away from the group.

At the conclusion of the song, the sprinklers shut off, returning to their resting places, while Grant knelt in front of Eliza.

A hush settled over every beating heart, so still and silent,

Penny could almost hear the water droplets trickle down the blades of grass.

"Eliza Lansbury Carter..." Grant's voice resonated with such ardent, all-consuming love, it appeared to take Eliza's breath away.

She gasped, covering her mouth with both hands as he withdrew the ring from an inside coat pocket.

"We've had our fair share of storm clouds, but when I look at you, all I see is the sun. You radiate this undeniable light—in your smile, the way you take care of others, your unrelenting joy. You make me a better man and a better father. And with you by my side, I'm not afraid to sing—and *dance*—in the rain, no matter how many thunderstorms come our way."

Holding up the sparkling ring with a dramatic flourish, he asked, "Will you do me the honor of being my wife?"

"It's about time," Eliza half cried, half laughed as she thrust out her hand.

After sliding the ring on her finger, Grant rose to his feet. "I assume that's a yes," he chuckled, his eyes filled with affection.

"Yes, but in case you're not sure..." Looping her arms around his neck, Eliza kissed him fiercely amid boisterous hoots and hollers.

As friends and family gathered around the newly engaged couple to offer congratulations, Penny slipped away to find Colt.

Emerging from behind the courthouse, he held a finger to his lips. "Shh... don't tell anyone about the hidden valve. It took me a few minutes to cover it back up."

"Your secret is safe with me," she promised, throwing her arms around him, drenched clothes and all. "You were pretty great out there, you know. If things don't work out at Jack's, you might have a career in showbiz."

He grinned, nuzzling his forehead against hers. "Glad you didn't change your mind after seeing my dance moves."

"Not a chance." She grazed his dimple with her fingertips,

marveling at how her entire life had changed in the span of a single summer.

"It's almost time for the fireworks," Colt pointed out, drawing her attention to dusk settling around them. "Mind if I catch a ride with you?"

"Actually..." She trailed off, her heart thrumming. "I have a better idea."

*

"*A*re you sure about this?" Colt asked, glancing over his shoulder.

Penny nodded, closing the visor of his spare motorcycle helmet.

After flashing her a devastating, dimpled smile, he revved the engine.

Penny encircled his waist with her arms and scooted closer, briefly mourning the added barrier of the bulky, padded jacket he'd asked her to wear for "safety purposes."

She smiled to herself, recalling all the ways they'd inadvertently influenced each other over the last several weeks. Neither one of them would ever be the same again. And if she were honest, she preferred the version of herself she glimpsed in Colt's eyes.

He saw her the same way her father had—beautiful and brave.

Colt gave her thigh a reassuring squeeze before revving the engine again, signaling the start of their next thrilling adventure.

As she nestled against him, her anxiety slipped away, replaced by a flutter of breathless anticipation.

And all at once, she realized that somewhere along the way...

Her happy place had ceased to be a place at all.

EPILOGUE

*B*ursts of red and blue sparks exploded in the night sky, reflecting off the shimmering surface of Willow Lake.

Oohs and aahs swirled around him, but Jack couldn't summon the same enthusiasm. Although the Bryant brothers outdid themselves each year with their elaborate fireworks display, an inexplicable hollowness in the pit of Jack's stomach kept him from fully appreciating each colorful crescendo.

Normally, Jack didn't mind his solitary, simplistic lifestyle. In fact, he preferred it. But as his friends paired off, one by one, he couldn't help wondering if they knew something he didn't.

He glanced at the contented couples all clustered together on the roomy quilt. Luke and Cassie, Grant and Eliza, and now Colt and Penny, too. In their close-knit circle, he and Reed were the last men standing.

"Just think," Cassie murmured, dragging Jack from his melancholy thoughts. "Frank could be getting down on one knee right now...."

"I hope not! Who's going to help him get back up?" Jack teased, then winced at his own ill-timed humor. He really needed to learn when to bite his tongue.

Colt chuckled. "It's actually pretty cool how much thought Frank put into the proposal. He doesn't exactly seem like the romantic type, but he really made an effort to make it special for Beverly."

"Love changes you," Penny purred with a soft, dreamy expression.

Jack shifted on his corner of the blanket, flinching as a pine needle managed to stab him through the thick fabric.

Why did people always espouse "love changes you" as if that were a good thing? Why couldn't love leave well enough alone? He *liked* being set in his ways. And he wasn't keen on anything— or any*one*—disrupting the life he'd made for himself. While it may not seem like much, it had come at a hefty price.

"Speaking of change," Penny said with a tentative tremor. "I have some pretty big news to share." While she addressed the group, her gaze flitted to Colt's face.

He gifted her with a warm, encouraging smile and squeezed her hand. "What is it?"

"I found out… I have a half-sister."

The loud *crack* of a firework exploding in the distance lent an audible exclamation to their collective shock.

"How'd you find out?" Colt gently drew her closer as she leaned into him.

"In a letter from my father that I hadn't opened until a few days ago." She hesitated as though she were still grappling with the revelation. "It took a while to wrap my head around it, but I've decided to reach out. We're only a few years apart, and… we're family."

"Do you know where she is?" Cassie's tone exuded empathy. Since she longed to find out the identity and whereabouts of her father, Jack knew she could relate in a way no one else could.

"No," Penny admitted. "But I have an idea where to start my search."

"My goodness," Eliza breathed. "What are you going to say if you find her?"

"I don't know exactly. I guess that I'd like a chance to get to know her. Maybe invite her to come visit for a while. Although, either Chip or I will have to share our bed. Unless I fix up Dad's room...." She chewed her bottom lip as though she wasn't sure how she felt about that idea.

Cassie turned to Luke. "We have a spare room. She can stay with us, can't she?"

"Of course." Luke's eyes warmed with affection for his wife.

"We have an extra room at the cottage, too," Eliza offered.

As everyone continued to chatter in excitement, already making plans for the mysterious sister, Jack experienced a curious flutter somewhere deep in his gut. Suddenly, his mind filled with a million unanswered questions.

What did she look like? Would she have Penny's red hair? Would their personalities be similar? Or complete opposites?

Was she single?

Whoa! Where did *that* come from?

Jack grimaced. He definitely didn't care about her relationship status. He didn't even know the woman.

Of course, maybe that's what he found so alluring.

If he did decide to give the whole *love thing* a try, getting involved with someone in Poppy Creek wasn't an option—everyone knew him too well.

But dating a stranger? That might work....

If he could keep her from uncovering the truth about his past.

Don't miss Frank's proposal to Beverly! Visit rachaelbloome. com/secret-garden-club to download the humorous, heartwarming bonus scene.

You can continue Jack's story and meet Penny's long-lost sister in *The Meaning in Mistletoe.*

ACKNOWLEDGMENTS

With each book I write, I still experience awe and wonder when I hold the final product in my hands. Countless hours—and, at times, it *feels* like blood, sweat, and tears—are poured into each manuscript. And it never ceases to amaze me how many people have a hand in the process.

For starters, I wouldn't have a single book published without the support of my incredible family. You guys are my biggest cheerleaders and have made so many sacrifices to make this dream come true. I am forever grateful.

Dave Cenker—you're not only a fabulous critique partner, you're a wonderful friend. And having a "writing buddy" who understands the marvelous, mysterious, and sometimes maddening creative process is a blessing and a treasure. And the fact that you share my love of alliteration is an added bonus.

Savannah Hendricks—without your insights, I would probably *still* be working on this novel. Thank you for getting me back on track.

Daria White—I am so grateful for your friendship and feedback over the years, and I look forward to growing in our careers together.

Gigi Blume, Elizabeth Bromke, and Melissa McClone—you ladies have blessed me with endless laughter, advice, and encouragement. I cherish our little community more than I can express. And Gigi, special thanks for your insightful critique and stunning book trailers—shout-out to your design service Sodasac Author Services.

Bob and Care—I treasure being able to include memories of Kay whenever possible, and I appreciate being able to pick your brains about certain details I've forgotten.

John and Lynn—incorporating tidbits from our Armenian side of the family means so much to me. And I thoroughly enjoy talking about the different coffee brewing techniques and delicious foods—not to mention sampling them during our trip to Lebanon!

Audrey McCord—our birthday "date night" watching *Singin' in the Rain* gave me the idea for Eliza's proposal, and now, I can't imagine it happening any other way.

And, as always, a thousand thank-yous to the brilliant team of professionals who turn my words into a finished product. Ana Grigoriu-Voicu with Books-design, each cover becomes my new favorite. And you nailed this one on the first try! Beth Attwood, somehow—with your magical editing skill—you manage to turn my bedraggled draft into a beautiful, polished manuscript. And Krista Dapkey with KD Proofreading, your keen eye and incredible knowledge—particularly when it comes to coffee—makes my prose sparkle.

And lastly, thank YOU, dear reader, for joining me in Poppy Creek for three books and counting. Your letters, emails, and comments mean the world to me. And sometimes, they even influence which story I'm going to write next...

ABOUT THE AUTHOR

Rachael Bloome is a *hopeful* romantic. She loves every moment leading up to the first kiss, as well as each second after saying, "I do." Torn between her small-town roots and her passion for traveling the world, she weaves both into her stories—and her life!

Joyfully living in her very own love story, she enjoys spending time with her husband and two rescue dogs, Finley and Monkey. When she's not writing, helping to run the family coffee roasting business, or getting together with friends, she's busy planning their next big adventure!

COLT'S CINNAMON & COFFEE STEAKS

For a slightly sweet, unexpected burst of flavor, try Colt's Cinnamon & Coffee Steaks. They pair perfectly with a savory side dish like roasted garlic potatoes.

INGREDIENTS

For steak marinade:

1 cup strongly brewed coffee, cooled to room temperature

2 tablespoons balsamic vinegar

2 tablespoons olive oil

2 tablespoons molasses

4 garlic cloves, minced

1 teaspoon salt

1 teaspoon black pepper

1 teaspoon paprika

1/4 teaspoon dried thyme

1/4 teaspoon ground cinnamon

2 sirloin steaks (approximately 2 pounds)

For caramelized onion topping:

Thinly sliced onion, in rings

1-2 tablespoons butter

Remaining marinade

INSTRUCTIONS

1. Combine marinade ingredients in a small bowl.

2. Place steaks in a large resealable bag, pour in the marinade, coating both sides of the meat.

3. Let sit in refrigerator overnight (ideally at least 24 hours).

4. Remove from refrigerator approximately 20 minutes before you're ready to cook.

5. Preheat the grill (steaks should sizzle when placed on top).

6. Grill steaks evenly on both sides until they reach your desired temperature (about 8-10 minutes for medium-rare).

For the topping:

1. In the bottom of a cast-iron skillet, lightly sauté the onion rings in melted butter.

2. Slowly add a few tablespoons of the remaining marinade, simmering until the onions soften and the mixture thickens.

3. Layer onion rings over steaks.

Serve with your desired side dishes.

Enjoy!

BOOK CLUB QUESTIONS

1. Do you consider yourself a more adventurous or cautious person?

2. Have you experienced any of the adventures on Penny and Colt's list? If yes, which one(s)?

3. Were you able to guess Leonard Davis's dying wish for Colt?

4. What did you think Timothy Heart's letter said before Penny opened it?

5. What do you think of the Robert Frost quote, "There is freedom in being bold?" Do you agree or disagree?

6. When did you first realize how the title was connected to the story?

7. Which character did you relate to the most?

8. What would you say is the overall theme of the novel?

As always, I look forward to hearing your thoughts on the story. You can email your responses (or ask your own questions) at hello@ rachaelbloome.com or post them in my private Facebook group, Rachael Bloome's Secret Garden Club.

Made in the USA
Coppell, TX
19 April 2021